P9-DCG-147

BLUE OF NOON

Georges Bataille
BLUE OF NOON
Translated by Harry Mathews

Urizen Books New York

Originally published in France in 1957 as **Le Bleu du Ciel**

©1957 Georges Bataille

©This translation Urizen Books 1978

All rights reserved

Printed in U.S.A.

Library of Congress in Publication Data

ISBN 0-89396-004-7

For André Masson

Contents

Introduction

I n London, in a cellar, in a neighborhood dive — the most squalid of unlikely places — Dirty was drunk. Utterly so. I was next to her (my hand was still bandaged from being cut by a broken glass.) Dirty that day was wearing a sumptuous evening gown (I was unshaven and unkempt.) As she stretched her long legs, she went into a violent convulsion. The place was crowded with men, and their eyes were getting ominous; the eyes of these perplexed men recalled spent cigars. Dirty clasped her naked thighs with both hands. She moaned as she bit into a grubby curtain. She was as drunk as she was beautiful. Staring at a gaslamp, she rolled round, irate eyes.

"What's going on?" she shouted.

In the same instant, like a cannon going off in a cloud of dust, she jumped. From eyes that bulged like a scarecrow's came a stream of tears.

She shouted again: "Troppmann!"

As she looked at me her eyes opened wider. With
long dirty hands she stroked my sick head. My forehead
was damp from fever. She was crying, with wild entreaty, the way one vomits. She was sobbing so hard her
hair was drenched with tears.

The scene that preceded this nauseous carnival —
afterwards, rats must have come crawling over the floor
round the two sprawled bodies — was in every way wor-
thy of Dostoevsky.

Drunkenness had committed us to dereliction, in
pursuit of some grim response to the grimmest of com-
pulsions.

Before being wholly affected by drink, we had
managed to retreat to a room at the Savoy. Dirty had
noticed that the elevator attendant was very ugly (in
spite of his handsome uniform, you might have taken
him for a gravedigger.)

She pointed this out to me with a distracted laugh.
Her speech was already awry — she spoke like a drunk
woman.

"You know —", racked as she was by hiccups, she
kept stopping short, "when I was a kid...I remember...
I came here with my mother. Here. About ten years ago.
So I must have been twelve.... My mother was a faded
old lady, sort of like the Queen of England... So, as it
happened, coming out of the elevator, the elevator man
— we just saw him —"

"Who — him?"

"Yes. The same one as today. He didn't stop it

level — the elevator went up too far — she fell flat on her face. She came tumbling down — my mother — "

Dirty burst out laughing, like some lunatic. She couldn't stop.

Struggling to find my words, I said to her, "Don't laugh any more. You'll never get through your story."

She stopped laughing and began shouting: "Oh, my, I'm getting silly — I'll have to... No, no, I'll finish my story. My mother. Not stirring, with her skirt over her head, that enormous skirt of hers. Like someone dead. Not another stir out of her. They picked her up and began putting her to bed. She started to puke — she was stewed to the eyebrows, except that one second earlier you couldn't tell — that woman... She was like a mastiff. She was scary."

I said to Dirty, abjectly: "I'd like to fall down in front of you, just the way she did..."

"Would you throw up?" Dirty asked me, without even a smile. She kissed me inside the mouth.

"Maybe."

I went into the bathroom. I was very pale. For no reason at all I looked at myself in the mirror for a long time; I was horribly unkempt, almost coarse, with swollen features that were not even ugly, and the rank look of a man just out of bed.

Dirty was alone in the bedroom. It was a huge room lighted by a multitude of ceiling lamps. She wandered around, walking straight ahead, as though she would never stop. She seemed literally crazy.

Her shoulders were bare to the point of indecency. In that light I found the glitter of her blond hair unbearable.

She gave me a feeling of purity nonetheless. Even in her debauchery, there was such candor in her that I sometimes wanted to grovel at her feet. I was afraid of her. I saw that she was worn out. She was on the point of falling down. She began gasping for breath, panting like an animal; she was suffocating. Her mean, hunted look was driving me insane. She stopped — I think her legs were squirming under her dress. There was no doubt she was about to start raving.

She rang the bell for the maid.

After a few moments, a redhaired, fresh-complexioned, and rather pretty maid came in. She seemed to gag on the smell. It was a highly unusual smell for so opulent a place: that of a lowdown brothel. Dirty had given up trying to stand on her feet unless she had a wall to lean on. She seemed to be in horrible pain. I don't know at what point in the day she had smothered herself in cheap perfumes, but in addition to the indescribable state she had gotten herself into, she gave off a sour smell of armpit and crotch which, mingling with the perfume, recalled the stench of an infirmary. She also reeked of whisky, and she was belching...

The English girl was aghast.

"You're just the person I need," Dirty announced, "but first you have to get the elevator man. There's something I want to tell him."

The maid vanished; Dirty, now staggering, went and sat on a chair. With great difficulty she managed to set down a bottle and a glass on the floor beside her. Her eyes were growing heavy.

Her eyes tried to find me. I was no longer there. She lost her head. In a desperate voice she called out, "Troppmann!"

There was no reply.

She got up and several times nearly fell. She made it to the bathroom door; she saw me slumped on a bench, haggard and white. In my drunkenness I had just re-opened the cut in my right hand. The bleeding, which I was trying to stanch with a towel, was dribbling rapidly onto the floor. Dirty, in front of me, was staring at me with eyes like an animal's. I wiped my face, thus smearing blood over my forehead and nose. The electric light was getting blindingly bright. It was unbearable, this light that wore out the eyes.

There was a knock at the door. The maid came in, followed by the elevator attendant.

Dirty slumped onto the chair. After what seemed to me like a very long time, her eyes lowered and unseeing, she asked the elevator attendant, "You were here in 1924?"

The attendant answered yes.

"I want to ask you — the tall old lady... The one who fell down getting out of the elevator and vomited on the floor... You remember?"

Dirty was articulating through dead lips, seeing nothing.

In fearful embarassment the two servants cast side-
long glances, questioning and observing one another.
"I do remember," the attendant admitted. "It's
true."
(This man, who was in his forties, may have had
the face of a thieving gravedigger, but it was of such an
unctuosity that it seemed to have been pickled in oil.)
"A glass of whisky?" Dirty asked.
No one answered. The two characters stood there
in deferential, painful expectancy.

Dirty asked to be given her purse. Her gestures
were so sluggish it took a long minute for her hand to
reach the bottom of the purse; as soon as she found the
stack of banknotes, she tossed it on the floor, saying
merely, "Go shares."
The gravedigger had found something to do. He
picked up the precious stack and began counting out the
pounds aloud. There were twenty in all. He handed ten
to the maid.
"We may leave?" he asked after a while.
"Oh, no, not yet. Please, sit down."
She seemed to be suffocating; blood was rushing to
her face. Showing great deference, the two servants had
remained standing; but they too became red and anxious, partly because of the staggering size of the tip,
partly because of the implausible, incomprehensible
situation.
Dirty remained mutely perched on the chair. There
was a long silence: you could have heard our hearts in-

side their bodies. I walked over to the door, pale and sick, my face smeared with blood; I was hiccupping and on the point of vomiting. In terror the servants saw that water was trickling across the chair and down the legs of their beautiful guest. While the urine was gathering into a puddle that spread over the carpet, a noise of slackening bowels made itself ponderously evident beneath the young woman's dress — beet-red, her eyes twisted upwards, she was squirming on her chair like a pig under the knife.

The trembling, nauseated maid had to wash Dirty, who seemed calm and content once again. She let herself be wiped and soaped. The elevator man aired the room until the smell had completely disappeared.

He then bandaged my cut to stop the bleeding.

Things were all back in their proper place. The maid was putting away the last articles of clothing. Washed, perfumed, more beautiful than ever, Dirty was stretched out on the bed, still drinking. She made the attendant sit down. He sat next to her in an armchair. At this point, drunkenness gave her the forsaken candor of a child, of a little girl.

Even when she remained silent, she seemed forsaken.

Occasionally she would laugh to herself.

"Tell me," she at last said to the elevator attendant, "during all the years you've been at the Savoy, you must have had lots of repulsive experiences."

"Oh, not all that many," he replied, although not

before finishing his whisky, which seemed to give him a boost and restore his composure. "The guests here are well-behaved, as a rule."

"Oh, well-behaved — that's a whole way of life, isn't it? Just like my departed mother when she took a tumble in front of you and puked all over your sleeves..."

And Dirty burst into dissonant laughter, to which, in that emptiness, there was no response.

She went on: "And do you know why they're all well-behaved? They're scared, do you understand? Their teeth are chattering — that's why they never dare let anything show. I can sense that because I'm scared myself — yes, my good man, I am. Can't you tell? Even of you. Scared to death —"

"Wouldn't Madame like a glass of water?" the maid asked fearfully.

"Shit!" Dirty curtly answered, sticking out her tongue at her, "I happen to be sick, don't forget that. I also happen to have a few brains in my head." Then: "You don't give a fuck, but things like that make me want to vomit, do you hear?"

With a mild gesture I managed to interrupt her.

As I made her take another swallow of Scotch, I said to the attendant, "Admit that if it was up to you, you'd strangle her."

"You're right," Dirty yelped, "look at those huge paws, those gorilla's paws of his. They're hairy as balls."

"But, Madame," the attendant protested, "you know I'm here to oblige you."

"What an idea! No, you idiot, I don't need your balls. I'm feeling sick to my stomach."

As she chortled, she belched.

The maid dashed out and came back with a basin. She seemed all servility, and utterly decent. I sat there pale and listless. I kept drinking more and more.

"And as for you — you, the nice girl," Dirty began, this time addressing the maid, "you masturbate, and you look at the teapots in shopwindows for when you'll set up housekeeping. If I had a fanny like yours I'd let everybody see it. Otherwise, one day you'll happen to find the hole while you're scratching and die of shame."

Appalled, I abruptly told the maid, "Sprinkle some water on her face — can't you see she's getting all hot?"

The maid immediately started bustling about. She put a wet towel on Dirty's forehead.

Dirty dragged herself over to the window. Beneath her she saw the Thames and, in the background, some of the most hideous buildings in London, now magnified in the darkness. She quickly vomited in the open air. In her relief she called for me, and, as I held her forehead, I stared at that foul sewer of a landscape: the river and the warehouses. In the vicinity of the hotel the lights of luxury apartments loomed insolently.

Gazing out at London, I almost wept, I was so distraught with anxiety. As I breathed in the cool air, childhood memories — of little girls, for instance, with whom I used to play at telephone and diabolo — merged with the vision of the elevator attendant's apelike paws. What was happening, moreover, seemed to me trivial and somehow ludicrous. I myself was empty. I was scarcely even capable of inventing new horrors to fill the emptiness. I felt powerless and degraded. It was in this uncompliant and indifferent frame of mind that I followed Dirty outside. Dirty kept me going; nevertheless, I could not conceive of any human creature being more derelict and adrift.

This anxiety that never for a moment let the body slacken provided the only explanation for a wonderful ability: we managed, with no respect for conventional pigeonholes, to eliminate every possible urge, in the room at the Savoy as well as in the dive, wherever we had to.

Part One

I know.

I'm going to die in disgraceful circumstances.

Today, I am overjoyed at being an object of horror and repugnance to the one being whom I am bound to.

My desire? Whatever worst things can happen to a man who will scoff at them.

The blank head in which "I" am has become so frightened and greedy that only my death could satisfy it.

Several days ago (not in any nightmare, but in fact), I came to a city that looked like the setting for a tragedy. One evening — I mention this only to laugh more cheerlessly — I was not alone as I drunkenly watched two old pederasts twirling as they danced (not in any dream, but in fact.) In the middle of the night the Commendatore *entered my room. That afternoon, as I was passing his grave, pride had incited me to extend*

him an ironic invitation. His unexpected arrival ap-
palled me.

Facing him, I started to tremble. Facing him, I
became derelict.

Next to me lay the second victim. The utter
repugnance on her lips made them resemble the lips of a
certain dead woman. From them dribbled something
more dreadful than blood. Since that day, I have been
doomed to a solitude that I reject and no longer have the
heart to endure. However, to renew the invitation, one
shout is all I need; and if I could trust my blind anger,
this time it wouldn't be me who exited, but the old
man's corpse.

Born of disreputable pain, the insolence that per-
sists in spite of everything started growing again: slowly
at first, then in a sudden burst that has blinded and
transfigured me with a happiness that defies all reason.

At this moment I am intoxicated with happiness.
Drunk with it.

I'll sing and shout it forth at the top of my lungs.

In my idiotic heart, idiocy is singing its head off.

I HAVE PREVAILED!

Part Two

Chapter 1 • *The Evil Omen*

During the period in my life when I was most unhappy, I used to frequent — for reasons hard to justify, and without a trace of sexual attraction — a woman whom I only found appealing because of her ridiculous appearance: as though my lot required in these circumstances a bird of ill omen to keep me company. When, in May, I came back from London, I was in a state of overexcitement, helpless, almost ill; but this strange girl didn't notice a thing. In June, I left Paris to meet Dirty in Prum; then, out of exasperation, Dirty left me. On my return, I was incapable of keeping up a presentable attitude at any length. I spent as much time as I could with the "bird of ill omen." However, I sometimes succumbed to fits of annoyance in her company.

This disturbed her. One day she asked what was the matter with me. (She told me shortly afterwards that she had felt I might go insane at any moment.)

1

I was irritated. I answered, "Absolutely nothing."

She was insistent: "I can understand it if you don't feel like talking. I'm sure it would be best if I left you now. You're not calm enough to give the project careful thought. But I want you to know that it's upsetting for me. What are you planning to do?"

I looked her in the eye, with no resolve whatsoever. I must have seemed at a loss, as if anxious to escape some obsession that would not be put off. She looked away.

I said to her, "I suppose you think I've been drinking?"

"No, why? Is that something you do?"

"Frequently."

"I didn't know that."

She thought of me as someone serious — wholly serious, in fact — and, for her, drunkenness was a thing that could not be reconciled with other obligations.

"It's only...You look worn out."

"Let's talk some more about the project."

"You're obviously too tired. You're sitting there as though you were about to keel over."

"That's a possibility."

"What's wrong?"

"I'm about to go insane."

"Why?"

"I hurt."

"What can I do?"

"Nothing."

"You can't tell me what's wrong?"

"I don't think so."

"Cable your wife to come back. She doesn't have to stay in Brighton?"

"No. As a matter of fact, she's written me. It's best for her not to come."

"Does she know the state you're in?"

"She also knows there's nothing she could do to change it."

The woman sat there puzzled. She must have been thinking that, insufferable and spineless as I was, it was her duty to help me out of my predicament. She finally made up her mind and said to me curtly, "I can't leave you like this. I'm taking you home, or to a friend's — whatever you like..."

I did not reply. Things at this point started going black inside my head. I'd had enough.

She took me home. I didn't utter another word.

2

I usually saw her at a bar-and-grill behind the Bourse. I used to make her eat with me. It was hard for us getting to the end of a meal. We spent our time arguing.

She was a girl of twenty-five, ugly and conspicuously filthy. (The women I previously went out with had, on the contrary, been pretty and well-dressed.) Lazare— her surname—suited her macabre appearance better than her given name. She was strange; indeed, somewhat ridiculous. It was hard explaining the interest I took in her. It necessarily implied some kind of mental derangement. At least, that's how it appeared to the friends I used to meet at the Bourse.

At the time, she was the one human being who could rescue me from dejection. When she came into the bar, her frazzled, black silhouette in the doorway seemed, in this fief of luck and wealth, a pointless incarnation of disaster; but I would jump up and guide her to my table. Her clothes were black, badly cut, and spotted. She seemed not to see what was in front of her; she frequently bumped into tables as she walked by. Her hair (short, stiff, unkempt, hatless) stuck out like crow's wings on either side of her face. Between these wings, her nose — that of a skinny, sallow-fleshed Jewess — emerged beneath steel spectacles.

She inspired uneasiness. She spoke slowly, with a serenity of mind to which all things were alien. Disease, exhaustion, poverty, and death did not matter to her. What she assumed in others was an utterly tranquil indifference. She cast a spell as much by her lucidity as by her visionary powers of thought. I used to give her the money she needed to print a tiny monthly review to which she attached great importance. In it she defended Communist principles that were a far cry from the official Communism of Moscow. Most of the time I thought that she was genuinely mad and that it was ill-tempered mischievousness on my part to keep playing her game. I used to see her, I suppose, because her frenzy was as unbalanced and sterile as my own private life and, at the same time, no less anxious. What most fascinated me was the unhealthy eagerness that prompted her to give her life and blood for the cause of the downtrodden. It would, I reflected, be the thin blood of an unwashed virgin.

3

Lazare took me home. She came in with me. I asked her to let me read a letter from my wife which I found waiting for me. The letter was eight to ten pages long. My wife said she couldn't go on any longer. She blamed herself for losing me; yet everything that had happened had been my fault.

The letter broke my heart. I tried not to cry; it was too much for me. I went to the toilet and cried by myself. I couldn't stop. When I came out I kept wiping away an endless stream of tears.

Holding out my soaked handkerchief, I said to Lazare, "This is pathetic."

"There's bad news from your wife?"

"No. Don't pay any attention. I can't control myself, but not for any particular reason."

"Nothing's wrong?"

"My wife told me about a dream she had..."

"What do you mean, a dream?"

"It makes no difference. You can read it if you like. It's just that you won't understand."

I handed her a page from Edith's letter. (I imagined that Lazare would understand it, but be astonished.) I said to myself: I may be obsessed with my own importance, but neither Lazare, nor I, nor anyone else can help that.

The passage I made Lazare read had nothing to do with what had so upset me in the letter.

"Last night," Edith wrote, "I had a dream that seemed never to end. It left me feeling unbearably oppressed. I'm telling you about it because I'm afraid to keep it to myself.

"We were together with a few friends, and someone said that if you went out, you'd be murdered. It was because of some political articles you'd written. Your friends insisted that it didn't matter. You didn't say anything, but you turned very red. You were determined not to get yourself murdered, but your friends were leading you on, and you all went out.

"A man then appeared. He'd come to kill you. To do so, he had to switch on a flashlight he was holding in one hand. I was walking next to you. The man, who wanted me to know he was going to murder you, switched on the flashlight. The flashlight fired a bullet that went right through me.

"You were with a young girl. At that instant I understood what it was you wanted, and I said to you, 'Since they're going to kill you, at least, while you're alive, take that young girl into the bedroom and do whatever you like with her.' You replied, 'I guess that's what I'll do.' You took the young girl into the bedroom. The man then said that the time had come. He switched the flashlight back on, firing another bullet. It was meant

for you, but I was the one who got it, and I realized that
things were all over for me. I touched my throat, warm
and sticky with blood. It was ghastly..."
    I had sat down on a sofa next to Lazare while she
was reading. I started crying again, although I tried not
to. Lazare couldn't understand why the dream was
making me cry.
    I told her, "I can't explain everything to you. It's
just that I've behaved like a coward with everyone I
love. My wife has devoted herself to me. She worried
herself crazy on my account while I was cheating on her.
Don't you understand — when I read about her dream
and think of everything I've done, I wish somebody
would kill me..."
    Lazare looked at me at that point the way one looks
at something that surpasses all expectations. This woman, who generally cast a steady, confident eye on everything, all at once seemed disconcerted. She didn't say
another word; it was as though she had been immobi-
lized. I looked straight at her. In spite of myself, tears
sprang from my eyes.
    I felt a paroxysm of giddiness, a childish need to
start wailing: "I ought to explain everything."
    I spoke in tears. Tears ran down my cheeks and be-
tween my lips. As crudely as I could, I told Lazare every
foul thing I'd done with Dirty in London.
    I said that even before that I'd cheated on my wife
in every possible way. I told her that I'd become so in-
fatuated with Dirty I could no longer put up with anything once I realized I'd lost her.

I told this virgin the story of my entire life. My telling it to a girl like her (she was condemned by ugliness to a stern stoicism and could only endure life ludicrously) was so impudent that it made me ashamed.

Never before had I told anyone what had happened to me. Each sentence was as humiliating as an act of cowardice.

4

I was to all appearances an unhappy man speaking contritely: but that was a fraud. Confronted with a girl as ugly as Lazare, I remained cynically disdainful at heart.

I explained to her, "I'll tell you why everything turned out so badly. It was because of something you're sure to find incomprehensible. I have never had any woman more beautiful or exciting than Dirty. She literally drove me wild. But in bed with her, I was impotent..."

Lazare hadn't understood one word of what I was telling her. She was starting to get impatient. She interrupted me, "But if she loved you, was that so terrible?"

I burst out laughing. Lazare once again seemed embarrassed.

"You must admit," I said to her, "that it would be hard to concoct a more instructive tale: two bewildered profligates condemned to nauseating one another. Still, it would be better if I started talking seriously. I don't

want to overwhelm you with details. But understanding
one another shouldn't be that difficult. She was as used
to excess as I was. There was no way I could satisfy her
with empty gestures."

(I was on the point of lowering my voice. I felt like
an idiot, but I needed to talk. Given my anguish, and no
matter how foolish it may have been, it was better for
Lazare to stay with me. She had stayed with me: I felt
less lost.)

I explained what I meant. "It's not hard to fathom.
I'd get myself into a lather. Time would be wasted making useless exertions. I'd end up in a state of physical exhaustion, but the psychological exhaustion was worse.
As much for her as for me. She loved me, but toward
the end she used to look at me stupidly, with an evasive,
even bitter smile. She was aroused by me, she aroused
me, but all we managed to do was nauseate one another.
Everything became impossible. I felt done for. At times
like that all I could think about was jumping in front of
a train . . ." I paused, then went on. "It always left this
taste of corpses —"

"What do you mean?"

"Especially in London. When I went to Prum, we
agreed that nothing like that should happen again. It did
no good. You can't imagine what levels of unnatural-
ness one can reach. I used to ask myself why I was impotent with her and not with the others. When I felt
contempt for a woman, a prostitute for instance, everything went fine. But Dirty made me want to grovel at
her feet. I respected her too much, and I respected her

precisely because she was irredeemably debauched. You must find all this unfathomable —"

Lazare said, interrupting me, "It's true I don't understand. In your view, debauchery degraded the prostitutes who earn their living by it. I don't see how that woman could be uplifted by it."

The hint of contempt with which Lazare had pronounced "that woman" left me feeling hopelessly entangled in nonsensicality. I looked at the poor girl's hands, at her grimy nails and the almost cadaverous hue of her skin. It fleetingly occurred to me that she had doubtless left a certain place without washing — no problem for other people, but to me Lazare was physically revolting. I looked her straight in the face. I was in such a state of anxiety that I felt as though someone were hunting me down. I felt that I was about to go somewhat insane. It was at once funny and ominous, as though there were a crow — a garbage-eating bird of ill-omen — on my wrist.

I thought, at last she can despise me with good reason. I looked at my hands: they were suntanned and clean. My light-colored summer clothes were spick-and-span. Dirty's hands most of the time were dazzling, with nails the color of wet blood. Why let myself be troubled by this creature, by this failure brimming with contempt for another woman's good luck? Obviously I was a coward and a flunky; but I was too far gone to feel any qualms about admitting it.

5

When, after a long wait, as if dazed, I answered her, all I wanted was to escape from unbearable loneliness with the help of this rather shadowy presence. In spite of her ghastly appearance, Lazare in my eyes barely had the substance of a shadow.

I told her, "Dirty is the one person in the world who has ever compelled my admiration." (In a sense I was lying — she may not have been the only one — but in a deeper sense it was true.) I added, "I was thrilled by her being so rich — then she could spit in other people's faces. One thing I'm sure of: she would have despised you. She's not like me —"

Spent with exhaustion, I tried to smile. Lazare, contrary to my expectations, endured my sentences without lowering her eyes. She had become indifferent.

I went on, "I'd just as soon get it all out, at this point. If you like, I'll tell you the whole story. At a certain moment in Prum I felt that I must be impotent with Dirty because I was a necrophiliac."

"What are you talking about?"

"Nothing extraordinary."

"I don't understand..."

"You know the meaning of 'necrophiliac'?"

"Why are you making fun of me?"

I was getting impatient.

"I'm not making fun of you."

"What's that supposed to mean?"

"Nothing much."

Lazare was hardly reacting at all, as though I were a presumptuous brat. She retorted, "Ever try it?"

"No. I never went that far. I had one experience — a night in an apartment where an elderly woman had just died. She was on her bed, just like any other woman, between two candles, her arms resting alongside the body (but with the hands left unclasped.) During the night there was no one in the room. That was when I realized."

"How?"

"I woke up around three in the morning. I thought I'd go into the room where the corpse was. I was terrified, but for all my quivering I kept standing there in front of that corpse. Finally I took off my pajamas."

"How far did you go?"

"I didn't budge. I was so excited I was out of my mind. It just came out of nowhere while I was watching."

"Was the woman still beautiful?"

"No. Completely shriveled."

I kept thinking that sooner or later Lazare would lose her temper, but she was now calm as a priest hearing confession. She simply interrupted me: "That's no explanation at all for your being impotent."

"It is. Or at least, while I was living with Dirty, I used to think it was the explanation. I realized, in any case, that my attraction to prostitutes was like my attraction to corpses. In fact, I'd read about a man who took his pleasure with them while they played dead between two candles, with their bodies whitened with tal-

cum powder — but that was beside the point. I spoke to
Dirty about things we could do, I started getting on her
nerves —"

"Couldn't Dirty play the part of a dead woman, if
she loved you? I can't imagine her stopping at a little
thing like that."

I stared at Lazare, astonished by her straightfor-
wardness in the matter. I felt like laughing.

"She didn't. Anyway, she's as pale as any corpse. In
Prum especially — she was more or less sick. One day she
even suggested I summon a Catholic priest. She wanted
to be given extreme unction while she went through her
death throes for my benefit. The joke seemed more than
I could bear. It was silly, of course; but mainly it was
appalling. We couldn't go on any more. One night she
was naked on the bed; I was standing next to her, also
naked. She wanted to needle me, and she began talking
about corpses — with no results. I sat there on the edge
of the bed and started crying. I told her I was a pathetic
idiot; I lay on the edge of the bed in a state of collapse.
She had turned livid; she was in a cold sweat. Her teeth
started chattering. I touched her; she was cold. Her eyes
showed nothing but white. She was a horrible sight.
Right away I began shaking, as though fate had seized
me by the wrist so as to twist it and make me scream. I
was so frightened I no longer cried so hard. My mouth
had gone dry. I put on some clothes. I wanted to take
her in my arms and speak to her. In her abhorrence for
me, she pushed me away. She really was sick. She
vomited on the floor. To tell the truth, we'd been drink-

ing all through the evening — drinking Scotch."
"Naturally," Lazare broke in.
"Why 'naturally'?" I looked at Lazare with loath-
ing. I went on, "That's how it ended. From that night
on, she couldn't stand having me touch her."
"She left you?"
"Not right away. We went on living together for a
few more days. She kept telling me she didn't love me
any less — on the contrary, she felt bound to me. But
she had this abhorrence of me, this insurmountable abhorrence."
"With a situation like that, you couldn't have
wanted it to last."
"I was incapable of wanting anything; but the
thought that she might leave me drove me wild. We'd
reached a point where anyone wandering in and seeing
us would have assumed there was a corpse in the room.
We came and went without uttering a word. We would
stare at one another from time to time — not often.
How could that have lasted?"
"But how did you separate?"
"One day she told me she had to leave. She didn't
want to say where she was going. I asked if I could go
with her. She answered maybe. We went together as far
as Vienna. In Vienna we rode by car to the hotel. When
the car drew up, she told me to take care of the room
and wait for her in the lobby — she had to go to the post
office first. I had the luggage taken in; she kept the car.
She went off without saying a word. I had the feeling
she was losing control. We had agreed long before to go

to Vienna, so I had given her my passport to pick up my letters; furthermore, all the money in our possession was in her purse. I waited in the lobby for three hours. It was during the afternoon of a day of violent wind, with low clouds, but so hot you couldn't breathe. It was clear she wouldn't be coming back again. I at once felt death approaching.''

Lazare, who had been staring at me, seemed touched at this point. I had stopped; it was she who asked me, out of humanity, to tell her what happened.

I resumed: "I had myself shown up to the room, with its twin beds and all her luggage. I can honestly say that death was boring its way into my head — I no longer remember what I did in that room.... At one point I went to the window and opened it; the wind was making a voilent noise — there was a thunderstorm on the way. In the street, right in front of me, there was a very long black streamer. It must have been a good eight or ten yards long. The wind had partly unhinged the flagpole; it seemed to be flapping its wings. It didn't fall. It made a big loud noise as it snapped in the wind at roof level, unfurling in twisted shapes, like a stream of ink flowing across the clouds. The incident may seem irrelevant to my story, but for me it was like having a sac of ink burst inside my head. That day I was sure of dying without further delay. I looked down, but there was a balcony one floor below. I took the cord used for drawing the curtains and wrapped it around my neck. It seemed sturdy. I got up on a chair, I fastened the rope, and then I started wanting to know how it would feel. I didn't know whether or not I would change my mind once I kicked over the chair. But I untied the rope and got down from the chair. I fell on the carpet in a heap. I cried until I hadn't a tear left. Finally I got up. I remember my head feeling heavy. I was absurdly cool; at the same time, I felt I was going crazy. I got to my feet with the excuse that I would squarely confront my fate. I went back to the window. The black streamer was still there, but rain was pouring down. It was dark, with flashes of lightning and a loud noise of thunder."

Lazare had lost interest in all of this. She asked, "What was this black streamer of yours doing there?"

I wanted to embarass her — perhaps talking about myself so obsessively had made me ashamed. I said to her with a laugh, "You know about the black tablecloth on the supper table when Don Giovanni comes in?"

"What has that got to do with your streamer?"

"Nothing, except that the tablecloth was black. The streamer had been raised in honor of Dolfuss's death."

"You were in Vienna when the assassination took place?"

"No, in Prum. But I arrived in Vienna the next day."

"Being there must have upset you."

"No." This foolish, ugly girl horrified me by the consistency of her preoccupations. "In any case, even if there'd been a war, it would have mirrored what was going on in my head."

"But how could war mirror anything inside your head? A war would have made you happy?"

"Why not?"

"So you think war could lead to revolution?"

"I'm talking about war, not about what it could lead to."

Nothing could have shocked her more cruelly than what I had just said.

Chapter 2 • *Motherly Feet*

I
1

began seeing less of Lazare.

My life was following an increasingly crooked path. I used to go to various places for drinks, walk around aimlessly, and finally take a taxi home. It was then, in the depths of the taxi, that I would think of Dirty and burst out sobbing. I no longer even felt any pain, or the least anxiety; inside my head, I was aware of nothing but absolute stupidity. It was like a state of perpetual childishness. I was shocked by the madness enacted by my wild state of mind whenever I had wanted to tempt fate, and I recalled the irony and courage I had shown; and, of all that, the one thing left was the feeling that I was some kind of idiot, extremely touching perhaps, but in any case ludicrous.

I still used to think about Lazare. It gave me a start every time. Exhaustion gave her a significance like that of the black streamer that had frightened me in Vienna. As a result of the few nasty words we had exchanged about the war, I saw in these sinister portents not only a threat to my life but a more general threat hanging over the world.... No doubt there was nothing real that could justify a connection between Lazare and a possible war. She insisted, on the contrary, that she loathed anything involving death; nevertheless, everything about her — her jerky sleepwalker's gait, her tone of voice, her ability to spread a kind of silence around her, her hunger for sacrifice — helped give the impression of a contract she might have drawn up with death. I realized that a life like hers could only make sense in a world and among men who were doomed to misery. One day the clouds in my head parted, and I immediately decided to rid myself of all the preoccupations I shared with her.

This unforeseen housecleaning had the same ludicrous side to it as everything else in my life...

Inspired by this decision and overcome with hilarity, I left my place on foot. After a long walk, I ended up at the Cafe de Flore among the sidewalk tables. I sat down with people I hardly knew. I had the feeling I was intruding, but I didn't leave. The others were discussing with the greatest seriousness all the recent events that it was *useful* to know about. To me, they all seemed to manifest, in addition to emptyheadedness, a most precarious reality. For an hour I listened to them without saying more than a word or two. After that I went to a restaurant on Boulevard du Montparnasse, to the right of the station. There, on the sidewalk, I ate the best things I could order and began drinking red wine —

much too much of it. By the end of the meal it was very
late, but a couple arrived — a mother and son. The
mother wasn't old; she was still attractive and slender,
with a most winning nonchalance about her. That was
of no interest, except that since I was thinking about
Lazare, she seemed all the more agreeable to look at for
being rich. Facing her was her very young, more or less
untalkative son, dressed in a sumptuous gray flannel suit.
I ordered coffee and started smoking. I was startled by
the sound of a wild cry of pain, as prolonged as any
death rattle. A cat had just leaped at another cat's
throat, at the foot of the shrubs bordering the terrace —
more precisely, under the table of the two diners I was
watching. The young mother stood up, uttered a sharp
shriek, and turned pale. She quickly realized that it was
a matter of cats, not human beings, and began laughing.
(She wasn't ludicrous, simply unaffected.) The wait-
resses and the owner came out onto the sidewalk. They
laughingly told us that this was a cat known for his exceptional aggressiveness. Even I laughed along with
them.

I then left the restaurant, convinced of being in a
good mood; but as I walked down an empty street, I
started sobbing. I couldn't stop sobbing. I kept walking
for such a long time that by the end I was far away, on
the street where I live. I was still crying at that point. In
front of me, three girls and two boys were noisily laughing their heads off. The girls weren't pretty, but they
were without any doubt frivolous and aroused. I left off

crying and slowly followed them as far as my door. Their clamor had aroused me to such an extent that, instead of going in, I deliberately retraced my steps. I hailed a taxi and had myself driven to the Bal Tabarin. At the very moment I went in, there was a swarm of virtually nude women on the dance floor. Several of them were pretty and unspoiled. I had asked for a table by the dance floor (I'd refused any other), but the place was full, and the chair I'd been given teetered on the edge of a raised section of the floor. I had the sensation that at any moment I might lose my balance and go sprawling among the nude dancing girls. I was red in the face; it was very hot; I had to keep mopping the sweat from my head with an already sodden handkerchief; I had difficulty raising my drink from the table to my mouth. In this ridiculous situation, my existence, perched on a precariously balanced chair, became the incarnation of misfortune; whereas the dancers on the light-flooded dance floor were emblems of unattainable happiness.

One of the dancers was slenderer and more beautiful than the others. She appeared with a smile like a goddess's, in an evening gown that clothed her in majesty. By the end of the dance she was quite naked, but even then she had an almost incredible elegance and refinement. The violet glow of the spotlights transformed her lithe, shimmering body into a marvel of ghostly pallor. I gazed at her naked behind like an ecstatic little boy, as though I had never in my life seen anything so pure, so scarcely *real* in its loveliness. When the game of undoing

her dress took place a second time, it left me so breathless and empty I had to hold on to my seat. I left. I wandered around, from cafe to street, from the streets into a
nighttime bus. Without meaning to, I got off the bus
and went into the Sphynx. I lusted after each and every
one of the girls who were tendered to all comers in that
place. It never occurred to me to go upstairs — I was
still bewildered by an unreal brightness. I then went to
the Dome. I was growing more sluggish all the time. I
ate a grilled sausage washed down with sweet champagne. It was refreshing, and very bad indeed. At that
late hour, there were only a few people left in that de-
grading place: the men were vulgar, the women old and
ugly. I went on to a bar where a woman who was common and barely pretty was sitting on a stool complaining
to the barman in whispers. I hailed a taxi. This time I
asked to be taken home. It was after four in the morning, but instead of going to bed and sleeping, I started
typing a report, leaving all the doors open.

     My mother-in-law, who had moved in with me to
be obliging (she looked after the place while my wife
was away), woke up. She called out to me from her bed,
shouting from one end of the apartment to the other
through her shut door: "Henri — Edith called around
eleven from Brighton. She was very disappointed not to
find you in."

     Since the day before there had, in fact, been a letter
from Edith in my pocket, saying she would call me that
night after ten. No one but a coward could have forgotten it. And I had actually been standing on my own door-

step when I went off again. I could imagine nothing more hateful. My wife, whom I had shamefully abandoned, had been worried enough to call me up from England; meanwhile, forgetting about her, I had been dragging my stupor and my rottenness from one vile place to the next. I started crying again as hard as I could. My sobbing had no point to it at all.

The emptiness was enduring. An idiot who soaks himself in alcohol and weeps — that was what I was ludicrously becoming. To escape the feeling that I was a forgotten outcast, the one cure was to swallow drink after drink. I kept hoping to get the better of my health, perhaps even of a life that had no justification. I had a notion that drink would kill me, but such ideas were vague: I might go on drinking and thus die; or I might stop drinking. . . . For the time being, nothing made any difference.

2

Outside Chez Francois, I emerged from a taxi rather drunk. Without saying a word, I went and sat down at a table among friends whom I'd come to join. It was the right sort of company for me — the sort that would steer me away from my self-obsession. I wasn't the only one who'd been drinking. We went for dinner to a cab drivers' restaurant. There were only three women present. The table was soon strewn with bottles of red wine, empty or partly empty.

The woman next to me was called Xenie. Toward

the end of the meal, she told me that she was just back from the country and that, in the house where she'd spent last night, she had seen a chamber pot in the bathroom full of some whitish liquid, and in the midst of it a drowning fly. Her excuse for speaking about this was her revulsion at the color of milk — for dessert I was eating a *coeur a la creme*. She was eating blood sausage and drinking all the red wine I poured into her glass. She swallowed the bits of sausage like a farm girl; this was affectation. She was just a girl with too much money at loose ends. In front of her plate I noticed an avant-garde magazine with a green cover that she was carrying around. I opened it and came across a sentence in which a country priest retrieves a heart with a pitchfork from a pile of manure. I was more and more drunk, and the image of the fly drowning in the chamber pot became associated with Xenie's face. Xenie was pale, and on her neck there were ugly tufts of hair, like fly's legs. Next to the breadcrumbs and splotches of red wine on the paper tablecloth, her white leather gloves were immaculate. The whole table was speaking in shouts. I concealed a fork in my right hand and slowly moved it over Xenie's thigh.

At that point, I had the bleating voice of a drunkard. This was partly acting.

I said to her, "You have a cool heart —"

I suddenly began laughing. I had just been thinking (as though there were anything remotely comic about it): "A *coeur a la creme*." I was starting to feel like throwing up.

She seemed depressed but replied appeasingly and without ill humor, "I have to disappoint you, but it's true. I haven't had much to drink yet. I wouldn't want to lie to you just to make you feel good."

"In that case — " said I.

Through her dress I dug the tines of the fork hard into her thigh. She let out a scream and, in her agitated attempts to get away from me, knocked over two glasses of red wine. She pushed back her chair. In order to see the wound, she was obliged to pull up her dress. Her underthings were pretty; I found the nakedness of her thighs attractive. One of the tines, sharper than the others, had pierced the skin. Blood was flowing, but it was a trifling wound. I didn't waste a second; she had no time to prevent my pressing two lips to her thigh and swallowing the few drops of blood I had just drawn. Somewhat taken aback, the others looked on with embarassed laughs. They saw that Xenie, pale though she was, was crying moderately. She was drunker than she had imagined; she kept crying, but she was leaning on my arm. I filled her knocked-over glass with red wine and made her drink.

One of us paid, and the amount was then divided up, but I insisted on paying for Xenie, as though wanting to stake out a claim on her. There was talk of going to Fred Payne's. Everyone crowded into two cars. The heat in the little place was stifling. I danced once with Xenie, then with women I never had seen before. I would step out for a breath of fresh air and persuade them,

one after the other (even Xenie, once), to join me for a
Scotch at the counter of a neighborhood cafe. From time
to time I went back into the nightclub; I finally stayed
put outside the door, with my back to the wall. I was
drunk. I kept staring at the passersby. For some reason
one of my friends had taken off his belt and was holding
it in his hand. I asked him for it. I folded it double and
amused myself by shaking it at women as though I were
about to strike them. It was dark. I no longer saw anything, no longer understood. If the women who went by
were with men, they pretended not to notice anything.
Then two girls came along, and one of them, confronted
with the threat of the raised belt, turned on me. She insulted me and spat her contempt in my face. She was
really pretty — blonde, with strong patrician features.
She turned her back on me in disgust and crossed the
threshold of Fred Payne's. I followed her among the
drinkers that had crowded around the bar.

Holding out the belt, I said to her, "Why are you
angry with me? It was for laughs. Have a drink with me."

She was laughing now, looking straight at me.

"All right," she murmured.

As though not wishing to be at a loss with this drunk
young man who was stupidly holding out a belt, she added, "Here."

In one hand she had a nude woman made of pliable
wax. The lower part of the doll was wrapped in paper.
She was carefully imparting a movement to the torso so
subtle that it was impossible to conceive of anything
more obscene. She was surely German — very bleached,

with a haughty, provocative manner. I danced with her
and said whatever foolishness came into my head. For
no reason, she stopped in the middle of the dance, struck
a serious attitude, and began staring at me. She was full
of impudence.

"Look," she said, and raised her dress higher than
her stockings: the leg, the stocking, the embroidered
garters, the undergarments — everything was sumptuous. She pointed at the bare flesh. She went on dancing
with me. I saw that she was still holding that awful wax
doll in her hand. It was the sort of novelty sold on the
way into vaudeville shows, where the barker drones a
succession of catch phrases, like "Sensational feel..."
The wax was soft; it had the suppleness and coolness of
flesh. After leaving me, she again held it aloft; and
while she danced a solo rumba in front of the Negro
pianist, she made it undulate provocatively, just the way
she was dancing. The Negro kept time with her at the
piano, laughing his head off. She was a good dancer.
People around her started clapping time. Then she took
the doll out of its paper cone, tossed it onto the piano,
and burst out laughing. The thing fell on the wooden
piano with the faint sound of a body flopping. The legs
had in fact flopped outward; the feet had been cut off.
The spread legs and the truncated little calves made you
wince, but they were fascinating too. I found a knife on
a table and cut off a slice of pink calf. My interim com-
panion grabbed it and put it in my mouth: it had a horrible, bitter taste of candlewax. I spat it out on the floor
in disgust. I wasn't utterly drunk. I was aware of what

would happen if I took this girl to a hotel room. (I had very little money left. I would emerge with my pockets empty, not to mention being insulted and overwhelmed with contempt.)

The girl saw me talking to Xenie and some of the others. No doubt she thought I had to stay with them and couldn't go to bed with her. She abruptly said good-bye and vanished. Soon afterward my friends left Fred Payne's and I followed. We went to Graff's for food and drink. I sat on my chair without saying anything; I was starting to get sick. I went to the washroom on the pretext that my hands were dirty and my hair needed combing. I don't know what I did. When a little later I heard someone calling "Troppmann," I was sitting on the toilet bowl with my pants down. I pulled up my pants and went out. The friend who had called me said that I had disappeared three quarters of an hour earlier. I went and sat down at the table with the others, but afterward they advised me to go back to the men's room: I was very pale. I went back; I spent quite a long time throwing up. After that, everyone said we should go home (it was already four.) I was taken home in the rumble seat of a car.

Next day (it was Sunday) I still felt sick. The day was spent in a state of atrocious lethargy, as if there were no more reserves to be tapped for staying alive. I got dressed around three, with the idea of calling on several people. I tried, unsuccessfully, to appear like a man of normal disposition. I came home early and went to bed. I had a fever, and the inside of my nose was sore,

as happens after prolonged vomiting. My clothes had
also been soaked by rain; I had caught a chill.

3

I fell into a sickly sleep. All night long, nightmares
and disagreeable dreams followed one another; they left
me completely exhausted. I woke up sicker than ever. I
recalled what I had just dreamed: on entering a large
room, I found myself in front of a four-poster canopy
bed — a kind of wheelless hearse. This bed, or hearse,
was surrounded by a certain number of men and women;
the same, apparently, as my companions of the previous
evening. The vast room was no doubt a theater, and
these men and women were actors or perhaps directors
of a production so extraordinary that I was filled with
anxiety as I waited.... I myself was to one side, in the
shelter of a kind of bare, dilapidated corridor: its rela-
tion to the room with the bed in it was like that of or-
chestra seats to the floor of a stage. The forthcoming
entertainment was evidently upsetting and full of out-
rageous humor: we were expecting a real corpse to appear. At that point I noticed a coffin resting in the middle
of the four-poster. The plank covering it disappeared,
gliding back as noiselessly as a theatre curtain or the lid
of a chess set; but what was revealed was not horrible.
The corpse was an object of indefinable shape — pink
wax of dazzling freshness. The wax recalled the blonde
girl's doll whose feet had been cut off. What could be

more delectable? It suited the sardonic, quietly delighted attitude of those present. A cruel and agreeable joke had just been played on some victim as yet unknown. Soon afterward, the pink object, which was both disturbing and appealing, grew considerably larger: it took on the appearance of a gigantic corpse carved in marble, with veins of pink or of yellow ocher. The head of the corpse was a huge mare's skull; its body was either a fishbone or an enormous jawbone that had lost half its teeth and been bent straight. The legs prolonged this spine the way a man's do. They had no feet — they were the long, gnarled stumps of a horse's legs. The sum of these parts was hilarious and monstrous and had the likeness of a Greek marble statue. The skull was topped by a soldier's helmet, which was set on its peak like a straw bonnet on a horse's head. Personally, I could no longer tell whether I was supposed to feel anxious or start laughing. It became clear that if I did start laughing, this corpse of sorts would be nothing but a sarcastic jest; whereas if I started trembling, it would rush at me and tear me to pieces. I lost track of everything. The recumbent corpse turned into a Minerva in gown and armor, erect and aggressive beneath her helmet. This Minerva was also made of marble, but she was running around like a crazy woman. In her violent way she was perpetuating the jest that had delighted me and nevertheless left me aghast. There was tremendous hilarity in the back of the room, except that no one was laughing. The Minerva started whirling a marble scimitar in the air. Everything about her was corpselike. The Moorish shape of her weapon referred to the place where things were happening: a "scimitary" of white marble, of livid marble. She was gigantic. There was no way of knowing if I was supposed to take her seriously. She became even more equivocal. For the time being, there was no question of her coming down from the room in which she was running around to the alley where I had fearfully taken refuge. I had now grown small. When she saw me, she realized that I was afraid. My fear attracted her. Her gestures became ludicrously wild. Suddenly she came down and started rushing at me, twirling her lugubrious weapon with ever wilder energy. Things were coming to a head. I was paralyzed with horror.

I quickly grasped that, in this dream, Dirty (now both insane and dead) had assumed the garb and likeness of the *Commendatore*. In this unrecognizable guise, she was rushing at me in order to annihilate me.

4

Before illness completely got the better of me, my life was a sickly hallucination from start to finish. I was conscious, but, as in a bad dream, everything passed before my eyes too quickly. After the evening spent at Fred Payne's, I went out in the afternoon in the hope of finding some friend or other who might help me back to normal life. It occurred to me that I could go and see Lazare at her place.

I was feeling awful. But the meeting was not what I

was looking for: it was like a nightmare, even more depressing than that dream, which was to take place the following night.

It was a Sunday afternoon. The weather that day was hot and airless. At her apartment on Rue de Turenne, I found Lazare in the company of a character who, when I laid eyes on him, gave me the silly idea that I might have to ward off the evil eye. . . . He was a very tall man who corresponded in the most painful way possible to the popular conception of Landru. He had large feet and a pale-gray cutaway too vast for his lanky body; here and there the cloth of the cutaway was worn and singed. His old, shiny trousers were darker than the cutaway and fell to the floor in corkscrews. His manners were exquisite. Like Landru, he had a bald head and a fine, dirty-brown beard. He expressed himself rapidly, in choice terms.

When I came into the bedroom, he was standing silhouetted in front of the window against a background of cloudy sky. He was a huge creature. Lazare introduced me, and said, as she named him, that he was her stepfather. (Unlike Lazare, he was not of Jewish blood; the mother must have been his second wife.) His name was Antoine Melou. He taught philosophy in a country *lycee*.

When the bedroom door closed behind me and I was obliged to sit down (exactly as though caught in a trap), I felt, as I faced those two individuals, more hampered than ever by nausea and fatigue. At the same time

I could imagine myself being slowly but surely mortified. Lazare had spoken to me more than once about her step-father. She said that from a strictly intellectual point of view he was the subtlest, most intelligent man she had met. I was horribly embarassed by his presence. I was sick at the time, and half out of my mind; I wouldn't have been surprised if, instead of speaking, he had let his mouth hang open — I imagined him letting the drool run into his beard without a word.

Lazare was irritated by my unexpected arrival; however, her feelings were not shared by her stepfather. Right after the introductions (through which he had stood unmoving and expressionless), he had no sooner settled into a broken-down armchair than he began talking.

"Monsieur, I would very much like to acquaint you with the details of an argument that has, I admit, left me in the depths of perplexity..."

In her restrained, distant voice, Lazare tried to stop him: "Dear Father, don't you feel that arguments like this are interminable, and that — that there's no point in tiring Troppmann? He looks exhausted."

With lowered head I stared at the floor by my feet. I said, "It doesn't matter. You can always explain what it's about without feeling obliged..." I spoke without conviction, almost in a whisper.

"Well," Monsieur Melou resumed, "my stepdaughter has just finished expounding the results of the arduous meditations that have literally engrossed her during the past few months. It seems to me, moreover, that the difficulty lies not in the extremely skilful — and, in my view, persuasive — arguments that she has utilized with a view to revealing the dead end into which history is being led by the events that are unfolding before our eyes..."

There was an excessive elegance in the inflections of the slight, silvery voice. I didn't even listen: I already knew what he was going to say. I was overwhelmed by his beard, by the dirty look of his skin, by his tripe-colored lips that were enunciating so well, while his large hands rose up to underscore his sentences. I gathered that he had acquiesced in Lazare's view and admitted the collapse of socialist expectations. I thought: they're in a pretty pickle, these two chumps with their collapsed socialist expectations.... I'm really sick....

Monsieur Melou went right on, articulating in professorial tones the "agonizing dilemma" that confronted the intellectual world in this deplorable age. (According to him, it was a misfortune for anyone gifted with intelligence to be alive just now.) Straining his brow into folds, he declared, "Should we wrap outselves in silence? Should we, on the contrary, bestow our help on the workers as they make their last stand, thereby dooming ourselves to an inescapable and fruitless death?"

For a few moments he remained silent, staring at the tip of his raised hand.

"Louise," he concluded, "leans toward the heroic solution. Monsieur, I don't know what you personally think of the possibilities now open to the movement for the emancipation of the working class. So allow me to set this problem *provisionally*" — at these words he looked at me with a knowing smile, stopping at length, like a tailor who steps back to get a better view of his results — "...in a vacuum. That's it, it's the only way to put it." He clasped his hands and rubbed them together very softly. "In a vacuum. As if we were faced with the givens of an arbitrary problem. Regardless of the actual givens, we always have the right to imagine the rectangle ABCD. In the present case, let us postulate, if you'll allow me, that either the working classes are ineluctably doomed to perish —"

I listened to those words: the working classes doomed to perish...I was far too distracted. The very thought of getting up and slamming the door on the way out was beyond me. I was looking at Lazare; I was in a stupor. Lazare was sitting in another chair, in an attitude at once resigned and alert: head bent forward, chin in hand, elbow on knee. She was scarcely less squalid than her stepfather, and even more dismal. She did not budge as she interrupted him, "No doubt what you mean is 'doomed to political extinction' —"

The huge geezer guffawed, chortled, and gracefully conceded, "Obviously! I don't posit their all perishing bodily —"

I couldn't help saying, "Why should I give a damn?"

"Perhaps, Monsieur, I failed to express myself —"

At which point Lazare's indifferent voice was heard, "You must excuse him if he doesn't address you as 'Comrade' — you see, it's a habit my stepfather picked up from his colleagues — in philosophical discussions..."

Monsieur Melou was unperturbed. He went right on.

I felt like having a piss. My knees were already fidgeting.

"There's no denying that we find ourselves confronted with a minute, disembodied problem whose very substance seems to elude us...." He looked disconsolate. He was racked by some difficulty only he could perceive. His hands initiated a gesture. "But its consequences cannot escape a mind as caustic and restless as your own."

I turned toward Lazare and said, "You'll have to excuse me, but would you show me to the toilet?"

For a moment she hesitated, not understanding, then rose and led me to the door. I had a long piss, after which I thought that I might be able to vomit. I exhausted myself in useless exertions, thrusting two fingers down my throat, making a dreadful sound as I coughed. I obtained some relief, however, and went back into the bedroom with the other two. I remained standing, somewhat ill-at-ease, and said straightaway, "I've considered your problem. But first of all I'm going to ask a question."

The workings of their features informed me that, no matter how astounded they might feel, my "two friends" would give me an attentive hearing.

"I think I have a fever." (I actually gave Lazare my burning hand.)

"Yes," Lazare said to me wearily, "you should go home and get into bed."

"All the same, there's one thing I'd like to know. If the working classes are done for, why are you both Communists, or socialists, or whatever?"

They stared at me, then glanced at one another. Lazare finally answered (I could barely hear her), "No matter what happens, we must not abandon the downtrodden."

I thought, she's a Christian. Why, of course! And I've actually come here...I was beside myself; I was outraged with shame.

"Why 'must'? What's the point of it?"

"One can always save one's own soul," Lazare whispered.

She uttered the sentence without moving, without even looking up. She gave me the feeling of unshakable conviction.

I felt myself grow pale. Once again I was feeling very sick to my stomach. I persisted nevertheless, "What about you, Monsieur?"

"Oh," Monsieur Melou muttered, his gaze lost in the contemplation of his scrawny fingers, "I understand your perplexity only too well. I'm perplexed myself — *fearfully* perplexed. All the more so since — since you have managed, in a few words, to isolate an unforeseen aspect of the problem.... Oh, my!" He smiled into his long beard. "Now here's something *fearfully* interesting. In fact, dear child, why *are* we socialist — or Communists? Why, indeed?"

He seemed to sink into unforeseen meditation. Little by little, from the summit of his immense trunk, the tiny head and its long beard began to droop. I noticed his bony knees. At the end of an uncomfortable silence he stretched out two interminable arms and sadly lifted them up, "Things have come to this. We're like a farmer working his land before the storm, walking down his fields with lowered head, knowing that the hail is bound to fall . . . .

"And then, as the moment approaches, standing in front of his harvest, he draws himself erect and, as I now am doing" — with no transition, this ludicrous, laughable character became noble: that frail voice, that slick voice of his was imbued with ice — "he pointlessly raises his arms to heaven, waiting for the lightning to strike him — him, and his arms. . . ."

As he spoke these words he let his own arms fall. He had become the perfect emblem of some dreadful despair.

I understood him. His discouragement was contagious. If I didn't leave, I would soon start crying again. I went out despondently, saying, almost in a whisper, "Goodbye, Lazare."

An unimaginable compassion then filled my voice: "Goodbye, Monsieur."

It was pouring. I was without coat or hat. It seemed to me that I didn't have far to go. I walked for nearly an hour, frozen by the rain that soaked my clothing and hair.

5

On the following day I had forgotten about this excursion into a demented reality. I woke up shattered. I was shattered by the fear I had experienced in my dream; I was haggard; I was burning with fever. I did not touch the breakfast that my mother-in-law set down at my bedside. I still felt like throwing up: the feeling had not really subsided for the past two days. I sent out for a bottle of bad champagne. I drank a glass of it iced. After a few minutes I got up to vomit. After vomiting I went back to bed; I felt some relief, but the nausea lost no time in returning. I started shivering; my teeth were chattering. I was obviously sick — sick in an extremely disagreeable way. I sank back into a kind of dreadful sleep: things all started becoming unstuck — dark, hideous, shapeless things that it was absolutely necessary to nail down. There was no way of doing this. My life was falling to pieces like rotten matter...

The doctor came and examined me from head to foot. He finally decided to come back with someone else. From the way he spoke I understood that I might be dying. I was in atrocious discomfort, I felt there was something stuck inside me, and I felt a violent need for relief; I didn't feel like dying the way I had on other days. I had the flu complicated with fairly serious pulmonary symptoms. Without realizing it, I had been exposed to cold during the rain of the previous evening.

I spent three days in a fearful condition. Except for my mother-in-law, the maid, and the doctors, I saw no

one. On the fourth day I was worse; the fever hadn't
gone down. Not knowing I was sick, Xenie phoned. I
told her that I was confined to my room and that she
could come and see me. She arrived a quarter of an hour
later. She was more natural than I'd imagined her — in
fact, she was extremely natural. After the spooks on
Rue de Turenne, she seemed human. I rang for a bottle
of white wine, explaining to her laboriously that I would
enjoy watching her drink wine — since I liked both it
and her — but I could only drink vegetable broth or
orange juice. She made no fuss about drinking the wine.
I told her that on the night I was drunk I had been drinking because I felt very unhappy.

She'd noticed as much, she said. "You were drinking as though you wanted to die. As fast as possible. I
would have liked to...But I don't like stopping people
from drinking, and then, I'd been drinking, too."

Her chatter was wearing me out. Still, it roused me
from my prostration to some extent. I was surprised
that the poor girl had that much understanding. But
there was nothing she could do for me — even if one
allowed that I might eventually emerge from my disease.
I took her hand, drew it toward me, and gently rubbed it
against my cheek so that it would be prickled by my
rough beard.

I said to her with a laugh, "You can't kiss a man
with a four-day bead!"

She drew my hand to her and kissed it at length.
She caught me by surprise. I didn't know what to say. I

tried to laugh as I told her (I was speaking very faintly, the way sick people do — my throat was sore), "Why are you kissing my hand? You know perfectly well that I'm fundamentally loathsome."

I almost wept at the idea that she couldn't help. The slightest obstacle was too much for me.

In reply, she merely said, "I know. Everybody knows you lead an abnormal sex life. It seemed to me that more than anything else you were very unhappy. I'm very stupid and I laugh a lot. There's nothing but dumb ideas inside my head, but since I met you and I heard people talking about your habits, I've been thinking that people who have loathsome habits, like you — it's probably because they're in pain."

I took a long look at her. She was looking at me, too, not saying anything. She saw that tears were streaming from my eyes, in spite of myself. She was not especially beautiful, but she was touching and natural; I would never have thought she could be so natural. I told her how fond I was of her; that, as far as I was concerned, everything was becoming unreal. Perhaps, when all was said and done, I wasn't loathsome, but I was done for. It would be best if I died now, which is what I was hoping for. I was so exhausted by fever and by this intensity of revulsion that I couldn't explain anything to her; in fact, I didn't understand anything myself.

With almost insane abruptness she then said to me, "I don't want you to die. I'll take care of you. I would have so much liked helping you live...."

I tried reasoning with her. "No, there's nothing you can do for me. There's nothing anyone can do...."

I said this with such sincerity, with such evident despair, that both of us fell silent. Even she didn't dare speak. At this point I found her presence disagreeable.

After this prolonged silence, an idea started inwardly arousing me — a stupid, hateful idea; as though all of a sudden my life was at stake; or, given the circumstances, more than my life. So, seething with fever, I told her in a tone of demented irritation, "Listen to me, Xenie." I began ranting, for no reason, I was frantic. "You've been involved in literary goings-on. You must have read De Sade. You must have found De Sade fantastic. Just like the others. People who admire De Sade are con artists, do you hear? Con artists!"

She looked at me in silence. She didn't dare speak. I went on, "I'm so irritated, I'm so infuriated, I'm so done in I don't know what I'm saying — but why did they do that to De Sade?"

I almost shouted, "Did any of them eat shit? Yes or no?"

All of a sudden I was wheezing so desperately that I had to sit up. As I coughed, I yelled in my cracked voice, "Men are hirelings. For each one who acts like a master, there are others who are bursting with conceit. And the ones who don't kowtow to anything are in jail or underground. Jail and death for some people means bootlicking for all the rest..."

Xenie gently pressed a hand against my forehead. "Henri, I beg of you" — as she bent over me, she was transformed into some kind of compassionate fairy, and I was scorched by the unexpected passion in her half-lowered voice — "don't talk any more. You're much too feverish to go on talking...."

Funnily enough, my sickly excitement gave way to calm; the strange, pervasive sound of her voice had filled me with semi-contented apathy. For a long while I looked at Xenie, not saying anything, smiling at her. I saw that she had on a navy-blue silk dress with a white collar, pale stockings, and white shoes. Under the dress her figure looked slender and pretty. Beneath the carefully combed black hair, her face was young. I was sorry I was so sick.

I said to her without hypocrisy, "I find you very attractive today. You look beautiful, Xenie. When you called me by my first name, it felt nice."

She seemed happy, in fact, out of her mind with joy; out of her mind with anxiety, too. In her agitation, she knelt down by my bed and kissed me on the forehead. I put my hand underneath her skirt, between her legs. I felt no less exhausted, but my discomfort had passed. There was a knock on the door, and without waiting for an answer the elderly maid came in. Xenie got up as quickly as she could. She pretended to be looking at a painting; she was acting like a madwoman, or perhaps a simpleton. The maid, too, was acting like a simpleton. She had brought the thermometer and a cup of broth. I was depressed by the old woman's stupidity, and I fell back into prostration. A moment earlier, Xenie's bare thighs had been cool under my hand; now, everything was teetering. Even my memory was teetering. Reality was falling to pieces. The only thing left was the fever: fever was burning away the life in me. I inserted the thermometer myself. I didn't have the strength to ask Xenie to look the other way. The old woman had gone. Xenie stupidly watched me rummaging around under the blankets until the thermometer at last went in. I think that as she watched me the poor girl felt like laughing, but her wanting to laugh brought her anguish to a head. She seemed at a loss. She stood there in front of me, with her hair undone, confused and quite red. Her face also bore witness to her sexual anxiety.

The fever was higher than the day before. I couldn't have cared less. I was smiling, but my smile was plainly a spiteful one. It was, in fact, so unpleasant to behold that the other person was at a loss to know what kind of a face to put on. Then it was my mother-in-law's turn to come in. She wanted to know my temperature. Without replying, I told her that Xenie, whom she had known for some time, would stay and look after me. If she wanted to, she could sleep in Edith's room. I said this disgustedly, then began smiling again as I watched the two women.

My mother-in-law hated me for all the suffering I had inflicted on her daughter; she was upset, furthermore, by any breach of propriety. She asked, "Don't you want me to cable Edith to come?"

I answered in a hoarse voice, with the indifference of one who can better control a situation the worse off he is, "No, I don't. Xenie can sleep here if she wants to."

Xenie was almost trembling as she stood there. She squeezed her lower lip between her teeth so as not to cry. My mother-in-law looked ridiculous. Her expression was one of circumspection; her bewildered eyes were frantic with apprehension — something most ill-suited to her listless posture. Xenie finally blurted out that she would go and get her things. She left the room without saying a word and without glancing at me, but I could tell she was holding back her sobs.

With a laugh I said to my mother-in-law, "She can go to hell if she wants to."

My mother-in-law rushed out to see Xenie to the door. I didn't know whether Xenie had heard or not.

I was the rubbish that everyone stamps on. My own malice was compounding the malice of fate. I had called down ill-fortune on my head, and here I was dying. I was alone. I was despicable. I had refused to let Edith be informed. A black hole now opened inside me as I realized that I would never again clasp her to my breast. All the tenderness in me called out to my little children: no answer would be forthcoming. My mother-in-law and the elderly maid were by my side. They would certainly look the part when it came to washing a corpse and tying up its mouth to keep it from hanging ludicrously open. I was feeling more and more irritable. My mother-in-law gave me an injection of camphor, but the needle was blunt and the injection hurt terribly. That was nothing; but what I had to look forward to was also nothing, aside from these ghastly little ordeals. Afterward, everything would disappear, even the pain; the pain then in me was what remained of a turbulent life. I foresaw something empty and dark, something unfriendly, huge — something that was no longer me.

The doctors appeared. I did not emerge from my prostration. They could listen and poke all they wanted. All I had left to do was endure pain, disgust, mortification — endure these longer than I could anticipate.

They hardly said anything; they didn't even try to force pointless words out of me. They would be back next morning. Meanwhile there was something I had to do. I had to cable my wife. I was no longer in a condition to refuse.

6

Sunlight was coming into my room. Through the open double-leaved window it was directly lighting up the bright red blanket on my bed. That morning, behind open windows, a soubrette was singing at the top of her lungs. In spite of my prostration, I recognized Offenbach's tune from *La Vie Parisienne*. The rollicking phrases of music burst joyously from her young throat:

Fair lady, do you recall
A man by the name of Paul
Stanislas, the Baron of Franscata?

In my condition, I imagined hearing a sarcastic answer to questions that were hurtling through my brain on
their way to disaster. Evidently inspired by lively elation,
the lovely idiot went on with her song (I had glimpsed
her once — even desired her):

One day, at the height of the fest-
    ive season, at my request,
A friend introduced us during the great regatta.
Did I love you? Of course I did!
Did you love me? I never once believed it...

Today, as I write, fierce joy has brought the blood
rushing to my head so crazily that I feel like singing
myself.

On the same day, Xenie (in the despair to which my
attitude had reduced her, she had resolved to spend at
least one night by my side) was about to enter the sunlit
room. I could hear the splashing sounds she was making
in the bathroom. Perhaps the young girl had not understood my last words. I felt no regret about them. I preferred her to my mother-in-law — at least I could briefly
enjoy myself at her expense. The thought that I might
have to ask her for the bedpan stopped me cold. I didn't
mind disgusting her, but I was ashamed of my position.

Being reduced to doing that in bed, with the help of a
pretty woman, and the stench — my heart sank. (Death
at this point inspired me with a nausea bordering on terror; and yet it was something I should have been yearn-
ing for.) The night before, Xenie had come back with a
suitcase. I had shuddered and started grumbling through
clenched teeth. I had pretended to be worn out, to the
point of being unable to utter a single word. When, out
of exasperation, I had finally replied to her, I began
shuddering with less restraint. She hadn't noticed a
thing. — At any moment she would be coming in, fancy-
ing that only the care of a woman in love could save me.
When she knocked, I managed to sit up (it seemed to
me that I was, for the time being, slightly better.) I answered, "Come in!" in a voice that was almost normal,
even a trifle solemn, as though I were playacting.

As she appeared, I added, less loudly, with tragi-
comic disappointment, "No, it isn't Death. It's only
poor little Xenie."

Wide-eyed, the delicious creature gazed at her pre-
sumed lover. Not knowing what to do, she fell on her
knees by the bed.

She softly exclaimed, "Why are you so cruel? I
would have liked so much to help you get well."

"Right now," I answered with well-mannered ami-
ability, "I'd like it if you just help me shave."

"Won't that tire you? Can't you stay the way you
are?"

"No. An unshaven corpse isn't a pretty sight."

"Why do you keep trying to hurt me — you aren't going to die. No, you can't die..."

"Think of what I'm going through meanwhile. If only everyone remembered in time...Once I'm dead, Xenie, you'll be able to kiss me all you want. I won't be in pain any more. I won't be so loathsome. I'll be yours and yours alone..."

"Oh, Henri! You're hurting me so terribly I don't know which one of us is sicker. You're not the one who's going to die, you know, I'm sure of that. It'll be me. You've brought me so close to death I'll never get away from it."

A short time passed. I was becoming somewhat distracted.

"You're right. I'm too tired to shave. You'll have to call a barber. Xenie, when I say you'll be able to kiss me, you mustn't get angry. It's as though I were talking for my own benefit. Did you know I have a perverted liking for corpses?"

Xenie was still on her knees, a step away from the bed, her features drawn: that was how she was watching me when I smiled.

At last she lowered her head and asked me in an undertone, "What do you mean? You've got to tell me everything now, I implore you. I'm afraid. I'm so terribly afraid."

I was laughing. I was going to tell her what I'd told Lazare. But this time things were stranger. I suddenly thought of my dream: in a flash, all that I had loved during my life rose up like a graveyard of white tombs, in a lunar, spectral light. Fundamentally, this graveyard was a brothel. The funereal marble was alive. In some places it had *hair* on it.

I looked at Xenie. With childish terror, I thought: *motherly!* Xenie was visibly suffering. She said, "Tell me. Now. Tell me — I'm frightened. I'm going out of my mind."

I wanted to speak; I couldn't. I made an effort. "In that case you'll have to listen to the story of my life."

"No, speak to me — just say something. But don't go on looking at me without saying anything."

"When my mother died —" (I felt too weak to go on. It abruptly came back to me: with Lazare, I had been afraid of saying "my mother". Out of shame I had said "an elderly woman.")

"Your mother? Tell me..."

"She had died earlier in the day. I slept at her place, with Edith."

"Your wife?"

"My wife. I cried and cried, shouting all the time. I ... During the night, I was lying next to Edith — she was asleep —"

Once again I felt too weak to talk. I felt sorry for myself. If I'd been able to, I would have gotten down on all fours and shrieked and called for help; there, on the pillow, my breath was as faint as a dying man's. . . . First I had told Dirty, then Lazare. I should have begged Xenie for mercy and thrown myself at her feet. I couldn't, but I felt a wholehearted contempt for her. She was stupidly going on with her moans and entreaties.

"Tell me. Show some pity for me — tell me..."

"I started down the corridor, barefoot. I was quivering. In front of the corpse I kept quivering — I was frightened and aroused. Aroused to the limit. I was in a kind of trance. I took off my pajamas. Then I — you understand ..."

I may be sick, but I was smiling. In front of me, her nerves shot, Xenie was lowering her eyes. She scarcely budged; but it was with a spasm, after a few interminable seconds, that she gave in, let herself go, and her body slumped limply down.

My mind wandered. I thought to myself: she's revolting — now's the time to go all the way. With difficulty I slid over to the edge of the bed. It required a sustained effort. I extended one arm, caught the hem of her skirt, and pulled it up. She let out a terrific shriek but did not move. A shudder ran through her. She was wheezing, with her cheek against the rug and her mouth open.

I was out of my mind. I told her, "You've come here to make my death even fouler. Now get undressed. It'll be like dying in a whorehouse."

Xenie sat up, leaning on her hands. Her deep burning voice came back to her "If you go on with this game," she said, "you know how it's going to end."

She got up. She slowly went and sat down on the window sill. She was staring at me without a tremor.

"See? I'm going to let myself go. Backwards..."

She actually began the movement that would have eventually tipped her into empty space.

I may be loathsome, but that gesture caused me pain. It added the fear of falling to everything that was already giving way inside me. I sat up. I felt harrassed. I told her, "Come back here. You know perfectly well — if I didn't love you, I wouldn't have been so harsh. Perhaps I wanted to suffer a little more."

She took her time stepping down. She seemed far away. Her face was shriveled with fatigue.

I thought of telling her the story of Krakatoa. My head had by now sprung a leak: every thought I had was drained away. I'd feel like saying something, then all of a sudden there'd be nothing for me to say.

The elderly maid came in, carrying a tray with Xenie's breakfast. She set it down on a little stand. With it she brought a large glass of orange juice for me; but my tongue and gums were inflamed, and I dreaded drinking even more than I craved it. Xenie poured out her hot milk and coffee. I held my glass in my hand, wanting to drink and incapable of making up my mind to. She saw that I was getting impatient. I was holding a glass in my hand and not drinking — a palpable absurdity. As soon as she saw this, Xenie wanted to relieve me of the glass. She leaped up, but so clumsily that she upset the table and tray as she rose. Everything went down in a crash of broken dishware. If at that moment the poor girl had had the slightest reaction, she might well have jumped out the window. With every passing minute her presence at my bedside was becoming more ridiculous. She felt that presence to be without justification. She squatted down, picked up the scattered pieces, and set them on the tray. In this way she was able to conceal her face; I could not see but only guess the anxiety that was contorting it. She finally used a bathtowel to mop up the rug, which was drenched with *cafe au lait*. I told her to call the maid and have her bring another breakfast. She didn't answer; she didn't look up. I realized that she was incapable of asking the maid for anything. Still, she couldn't go without food.

I said to her, "Open the cupboard. You'll find a tin box with cookies in it. There should be a bottle of champagne that's nearly full. It'll be warm — just the same, if you feel like it —"

Opening the cupboard and turning her back to me, she began eating the cookies. Then, since she was thirsty, she helped herself to champagne and quickly drank it down. She hurriedly ate some more, helped herself to another glass, and finally shut the door. She finished straightening up. She was at an utter loss — she had no idea what to do. I was supposed to be given an injection of camphor oil. I told her about it. She got things ready in the bathroom and went off to the kitchen for whatever was needed. After a few minutes she came back with a full hypodermic. I had some trouble turning face down. After pulling down my pajama bottom I presented her with one buttock. She said she didn't know how to manage.

"In that case," I told her, "you'll hurt me. You'd better ask my mother-in-law —"

Without further ado she resolutely inserted the needle. No one could have conceivably managed any better. The presence of this girl who had just stuck the needle into my buttock was becoming more and more disconcerting. I succeeded in turning over, not without difficulty. I had no modesty left. She helped me pull up my pajamas. I hoped she'd go on drinking. I wasn't feeling so awful. I told her she should take the bottle and a glass from the cupboard, put them by her side, and keep drinking.

She simply said, "Whatever you like."

I thought, if she keeps it up, if she keeps drinking, I'll tell her 'Lie down' and she'll lie down, or 'Lick the table' and she'll lick the table. . . .

My death was going to be magnificent.

There was nothing that wasn't loathsome to me. Thoroughly loathsome.

I asked Xenie, "Do you know a song that begins, 'I dreamt of a flower'?"

"Yes — why?"

"I'd like you to sing it to me. — You're lucky being able to drink, even bad champagne. Have some more. You can't leave a bottle half empty."

"Whatever you like."

She took several long swigs.

I went on, "What's there to stop you from singing?"

"Why 'I dreamt of a flower'?"

"Because."
"Oh, well. That or anything else."
"You will sing, won't you? Let me kiss your hand. You're sweet."

Resignedly she started to sing. She was standing up, her hands empty, her eyes glued to the floor.

> I dreamt of a flower
> That would never die,
> I dreamt of a love
> That would never fade

Her low voice rose up with great feeling, biting off the last words to end on a note of heartrending weariness:

> Ah, why in this world through which we stray
> Must flowers and happiness bloom but a day?

Then I said to her, "There's something you can do for me."
"I'll do whatever you want."
"It would have been so wonderful if you'd been naked when you sang to me."
"Naked?"
"Have another drink. You can lock the door. I'll leave room for you next to me, in my bed. Now get undressed."
"But it's crazy."

"Remember what you said. You'll do whatever I like."

I said nothing more but looked at her as if I loved her. She went on slowly drinking. She looked at me. Then she took off her dress. She was almost insanely in-genuous. She unhesitatingly removed her slip. I told her that in the recess at the far end of the room she'd find one of my wife's bathrobes among the clothes hanging there. She could slip into it if she had to, in case some-one appeared. She could keep on her stockings and shoes and hide the dress and slip she'd just taken off.

I then said, "I want you to sing to me one last time. Then you can lie down next to me."

I was, in fact, aroused: the more so since her body was prettier and younger than her face; most of all be-cause, in her stockings, she was so oppressively nude.

I told her again, this time almost in a whisper. It was a kind of entreaty. I leaned toward her. I used my unsteady voice to feign ardent love, "Please, please stand up and sing. Sing your head off —"

"If you like," said she.

She was so unsettled by love and the sense of her nakedness that her voice shrank in her throat. The peri-ods of the song warbled through the room. Her whole body seemed ablaze. The drunken, singing head shook with some delirious impulse that seemed to be destroy-ing her. What insanity! She was weeping, in her wild nakedness, as she approached my bed, which to me was a death bed. She fell on her knees, she fell down in front of me and hid her tears in the sheets.

I said to her, "Stretch out next to me, and don't cry any more...."

She replied: "I'm drunk."

The bottle on the table was empty. She got into bed. She still had her shoes on. She lay down, fanny upwards, and buried her head in the bolster. It was so strange speaking into her ear with the ardent tenderness that usually manifests itself only at night.

I told her very softly, "Don't cry any more. I just had to have you act crazy. I needed it so as not to die."

"You won't die — honest?"

"I don't want to die any more. I want to live with you. When you got up on the window sill I was afraid of death. Thinking of that empty window — I was terribly afraid. You, then me: two people dead, and the room empty..."

"Wait — if you like, I'll go shut the window."

"No, don't bother. Stay next to me. Nearer than that — I want to feel your breath."

She moved closer, but her mouth had a winy smell. She said to me, "You're burning."

"I feel worse," I resumed. "I'm afraid of dying. All my life I've been obsessed with the fear of death, and now — I can't stand seeing that window open any longer, it's making me dizzy. That's what it is."

Xenie immediately jumped up.

"Go ahead and shut it, but come back. Come back right away —"

Everything was becoming confused. Sometimes, in similar fashion, sleep will irresistibly prevail.... No point talking: words would already be dead and inert, the way they are in dreams.

I stammered, "He can't get in —"

"Who do you mean? Get in?"

"I'm afraid."

"Whom are you frightened of?"

"...Frascata..."

"Frascata?"

"No. I was dreaming. There's somebody else —"

"Not your wife —"

"No, Edith can't be here yet, it's too soon..."

"Then who else, Henri? Whom were you talking about? You've got to tell me, I'm going crazy — you know I've had too much to drink...." ·

After a painful silence, I announced, "No one's coming!"

A tormented shadow abruptly fell out of the sunny sky, shaking and snapping in the window frame. Shrinking and trembling I withdrew inside myself. It was a long rug tossed down from the floor above. For one brief moment I trembled: in my daze I thought that the man I call the *Commendatore* had come in. He would appear whenever I invited him. Even Xenie had been frightened. Like me, she felt apprehensive about a window where she had just been sitting for the purpose of jumping out of it. At the moment of the rug's intrusion, she hadn't screamed — she had curled up against me, pale, with eyes like a madwoman's.

I was getting out of my depth.

"It's too dark..."

...Xenie stretched out alongside me — it was then she assumed the appearance of a dead woman.... She was naked.... She had the pale breasts of a prostitute....

A sooty cloud was blackening the sky...making off with the sky and the light inside me.

Was I to die with a corpse at my side?

...Even this farce was too much for me...it was just a farce....

Chapter 3 · *Antonio's Story*

1

A few weeks later, I had actually forgotten being sick. In Barcelona I ran into Michel. I suddenly found him in front of me, sitting at a table at the Criolla. Lazare had told him I was going to die. Michel's words were a painful reminder of the past.

I ordered a bottle of brandy. I started drinking, and I kept Michel's glass filled. It didn't take me long to get drunk. I'd known for a long time about the Criolla's main attraction; it held little charm for me. A boy in girl's clothing was performing a number on the dance floor. The dress he was wearing left his back bare to the buttocks. The heel-drum of Spanish dancing resounded on the boards....

I felt deeply ill-at ease. I looked at Michel. He wasn't accustomed to perversion. As he himself got drunk, Michel's awkwardness increased. He was fidgeting in his chair.

I was exasperated. I said to him, "I wish Lazare could see you — in a dive!"

In his surprise he cut me short: "But Lazare often comes to the Criolla."

I turned toward Michel with an innocent air of bewilderment.

"It's true. Lazare stayed in Barcelona last year, and she often spent her nights at the Criolla. Is that so extraordinary?"

The Criolla is, of course, one of the better known curiosities of Barcelona. I nevertheless thought that Michel was joking. I told him so; the joke was silly. The mere thought of Lazare made me sick. As I resisted my anger, I felt it welling up inside me.

I shouted. I was insane. I'd picked up the bottle in one hand. "Michel, if Lazare was here in front of me, I'd kill her."

Another dancer — another boy-as-girl — made his entrance accompanied by shouting and outbursts of laughter. He had a blond wig. He was gorgeous, hideous, and ludicrous.

"I'd like to beat her and hit her — "

It was so preposterous that Michel stood up. He took me by the arm. He was frightened — I was losing all control, and he himself was drunk. As he slumped back into his chair, he looked forlorn.

I composed myself and started looking at the dancer with the sunlike tresses.

"But Lazare isn't the one who behaved badly,"

Michel exclaimed. "She told me that you, on the other hand, had severely mistreated her — verbally — "

"She told you that?"

"But she doesn't hold it against you."

"Just don't keep telling me that she's been to the Criolla. Lazare at the Criolla...!"

"She's come here with me several times. She found it highly interesting. I couldn't get her out. She must have been astonished. She never once mentioned the silly things you said to her."

I was pretty much calmed down. "I'll tell you about it some other time. She came to see me when I was at death's door. So she doesn't hold it against me? Well, I'll never forgive her. *Never*, do you understand? Anyway, would you be good enough to tell me what brought her to the Criolla? *Lazare?*"

I was incapable of imagining Lazare seated where I was, watching a disreputable show. I was in a daze. I had the feeling that I'd forgotten something — I'd known what it was a second earlier, and I absolutely had to recall it. I felt like speaking with greater thoroughness. I felt like speaking louder. I was aware of my utter helplessness. I was getting completely drunk.

In his concern, Michel became more and more awkward. He was sweating and miserable. The more he pondered, the more beyond him everything seemed.

"I tried to twist her wrist," he said.

". . . ."

"Once. Right here."

I was undergoing heavy stress. I felt on the point of exploding.

In the midst of the tumult, Michel guffawed, "You don't know what she's like. She wanted me to stick pins into her skin. You don't know what she's like. She's unbearable!"

"Why pins?"

"She wanted to be prepared."

"For what?" I shouted. "Prepared?"

Michel laughed louder than ever. "For withstanding torture..."

Once again he turned serious, as well as he could — abruptly and awkwardly. He looked hurried; he looked idiotic. He lost no time speaking. He was in a fury, "There's something else you absolutely have to know. Lazare, you know, casts a spell on anyone who listens to her. She seems like someone from another world. There are people here, workers, who felt ill-at-ease with her. They admired her, then they ran into her at the Criolla. Here at the Criolla she looked like a spook. Her friends — they were sitting at the same table — were appalled. They couldn't understand her being here. One day, one of them started drinking, in exasperation. He lost his head. He ordered a bottle, just the way you did. He emptied glass after glass. I thought he'd end up in bed with her. He certainly could have killed her — he would have preferred getting killed *for* her, but he never would have asked her to go to bed with him. He found her captivating. He'd never have understood if I'd talked about her ugliness. But in his eyes Lazare was a saint — and a saint, moreover, she should remain. He was a very young mechanic; his name was Antonio."

I did as the young worker had done and emptied my glass. Michel, who rarely drank, was keeping up with me. He fell into a state of violent excitement. I, for my part, was gazing through the blinding light into vacancy, into an exorbitance beyond our grasp.

Michel wiped the sweat from his forehead. He went on, "Lazare was irritated to see him drinking. She looked him in the eye and told him, 'I gave you a paper to sign this morning, and you signed without reading it.' She spoke without a trace of irony. Antonio replied, 'What's the difference?' Lazare retorted, 'What if I'd given you a declaration of Fascist beliefs to sign?' Antonio in turn looked at Lazare and stared into her eyes. He was fascinated but out of control. He replied in deliberate tones, 'I'd kill you.' Lazare asked him, 'Are you carrying a revolver?' He answered, 'Yes.' Lazare said, 'Let's go outside.' We went outside. They wanted a witness."

By now I was having a hard time breathing. I asked Michel, who was slowing down, to proceed without delay. Once again he wiped the sweat from his brow, "We went over to the waterfront, at the point where there are steps leading down. Day was breaking. We walked without saying a word. I was bewildered, Antonio was in a cold fury and stupefied with drink, Lazare was as calm and far away as someone dead...!"

"But was it a joke?"

"It was no joke. I didn't intervene. I don't know why I felt such anxiety. At the waterfront, Lazare and Antonio climbed down to the lowermost steps. Lazare asked Antonio to take out the revolver and hold the barrel against her chest."

"Did Antonio do it?"

"He seemed far away himself. He took a Browning out of his pocket, cocked it, and held the barrel against Lazare's chest."

"And then?"

"Lazare asked him, 'Aren't you going to shoot?' He didn't answer. For two minutes he didn't budge. Finally he said 'No' and lowered the revolver."

"That's all?"

"Antonio looked worn-out. He was pale. Since it was chilly, he started shivering. Lazare took the revolver and extracted the first cartridge. This cartridge had been in the barrel when it was resting against her chest. Then she spoke to Antonio. She said to him, 'Let me have it.' She wanted to keep it as a souvenir."

"Did Antonio let her keep it?"

"Antonio said to her, 'Whatever you like.' She put the cartridge in her handbag."

Michel fell silent. He seemed less at ease than ever. I thought of the fly in milk. He no longer knew whether to laugh or break down. He truly reminded me of a fly in milk, or perhaps a bad swimmer swallowing water. He couldn't hold his liquor. By the end he was on the verge of tears. He was gesticulating strangely in the midst of the music, as though he had to get rid of some insect.

"Have you ever heard a sillier story?" he added.

It was the sweat running off his forehead that had prompted his gesticulations.

2

The story had left me stunned.

I managed to ask Michel, as though we weren't drunk but obliged to remain desperately alert (in spite of everything, our heads were clear), "Can you tell me what Antonio was like?"

Michel pointed to a young boy at a nearby table and said that he looked like him.

"Antonio? He had a quick-tempered way about him. Two weeks ago they arrested him. He was an agitator."

I went on questioning him as gravely as I could. "Can you describe the political situation in Barcelona to me? I don't know a thing."

"It'll all blow sky-high..."

"Why hasn't Lazare come?"

"We're expecting her any day."

So Lazare was coming to Barcelona to take part in the agitation. My state of helplessness had become so intolerable that without Michel the night might have come to a bad end.

Michel's own head may have been screwed on backwards, but he managed to make me sit down again. I was trying — not without difficulty — to recall Lazare's tone of voice. A year ago she had been sitting in one of these chairs.

Lazare always used to speak imperturbably and slowly, in an innermost tone of voice. It made me laugh whenever I thought of any of the slow-spoken sentences I had heard. I wished I'd been Antonio. I would have killed her. The thought that perhaps I loved Lazare drew a shout from me that was lost in the hubbub. I felt capable of biting myself. I was obsessed by the revolver, by the need to shoot, to empty the chamber — into her belly, into her... As though I were tumbling through space and making silly gestures, the way we fire ineffectual shots in dreams.

I had had enough. To compose myself, I had to make a great effort. I told Michel, "Lazare revolts me so much that it scares me."

Across the table, Michel looked sick. He too was making a superhuman effort to hold onto himself. He rested his forehead in his hands, unable to stifle a weak laugh, "Yes, according to her, you seemed to hate her so violently... Even she was afraid. I hate her myself."

"*You* hate her! Two months ago she came to see me in bed, when she thought I was going to die. She was shown in, and she started toward my bed on tiptoe. When I spied her in the middle of the room, she stopped, still on tiptoe, motionless. She looked like a scarecrow standing motionless in the middle of a field. . . .

"Three steps away from me, she was as pale as if she were looking at a corpse. There was sunlight in the room, but Lazare was dark. Dark the way prisons are dark. She was attracted by death, can you understand that? When I suddenly laid eyes on her, I was so frightened I screamed."

"But what about her?"

"She didn't say a word. She didn't budge. I shouted abuse at her. I told her she was a filthy asshole. I said she had the mind of a priest. I even managed to tell her that I was calm and composed. But I was shaking in every limb. I told her that dying was painful enough, but that having to behold such an abject creature while dying was too much. I was sorry my bedpan wasn't full — I would have chucked the shit in her face."

"What did she say?"

"She told my mother-in-law, without raising her voice, that it would be best if she left."

I kept laughing and laughing. I was seeing double. I was losing my head.

It was Michel's turn to guffaw, "She left?"

"She left. My sheets were drenched with sweat. I thought I was going to die then and there. But by the end of the day I was better, I felt that I was out of danger. Get this straight: I certainly frightened her. Otherwise, don't you agree, I'd be dead!"

Michel, who had slumped down, sat up again. He

was feeling awful, but he also had the look of one who has just quenched his thirst for revenge. He was raving. "Lazare loves little birds. So she says. But she's lying. Lying, do you hear? She reeks of the grave. I know — I took her in my arms one day..."

Michel stood up. He was dead white. With an expression of profound stupidity he said, "I'd better go to the bathroom."

I too stood up. Michel went away to vomit. I stood there, with all the cries of the Criolla inside my head, lost in the crush. I no longer understood. Had I shouted, no one would have heard, not even had I shouted my head off. I had nothing to say. I was still doomed to go astray. I kept laughing. I would have liked to spit in the other people's faces.

Chapter 4 • *The Blue of Noon*

A
                    1

s I woke up, panic gripped me — at the thought of confronting Lazare. I dressed quickly and went out to wire Xenie to join me in Barcelona. Why had I left Paris without going to bed with her? I'd put up with her, with some difficulty, during the entire time I was sick; and yet, if one makes love with a woman one is scarcely in love with, she becomes more bearable. I'd had enough of making love with prostitutes.

My dread of Lazare was a shameful one: as though I owed her some sort of explanation. I recalled the absurd feeling that had overcome me at La Criolla. The thought of running into her filled me with such dread that I no longer felt hatred for her. I got out of bed and dressed hastily in order to send the telegram. I had, in my despair, been happy for nearly a month. I'd been emerging from a nightmare; now the nightmare was catching up with me.

In my telegram I explained to Xenie that until now I had had no fixed address. I wanted her to come to Barcelona as fast as she could.

I had an appointment with Michel. He seemed worried. I took him out to lunch at a little restaurant on the Parallelo. He ate little and drank even less. I told him that I didn't read the papers. He said, not without irony, that a general strike had been called for the following day. I'd be better off going to Calella where I could join my friends. I, on the other hand, was determined to remain in Barcelona and witness the disturbances, should there be any. I didn't want to become involved, but I did have a car at my disposition. One of my friends then staying at Calella had lent it to me for a week. If he needed a car, I could act as his driver. He burst into frankly hostile laughter. He was sure of belonging to a different world: he was penniless, and he was ready for anything that might help the revolution. It occurred to me that in a riot, he would, as usual, have his head in the clouds and stupidly get himself killed. I disliked the entire business. In a sense, the revolution was part of the nightmare from which I thought I'd escaped. It was not without a feeling of embarassment that I remembered the night spent at La Criolla, or Michel himself. That night, I imagined, must have bothered him, not only bothered but oppressed him. His voice took on an indefinable quality of provocation and anxiety when, at last, he told me that Lazare had arrived the night before.

Confronted with Michel, and especially with his smiles, I maintained an air of indifference — even though the abruptness of the announcement was enough to have disconcerted me. I told him that there was no way for me to become a native worker, rather than a rich Frenchman in Catalonia for his own pleasure. But a car could be useful in certain cases, even when the circumstances were as risky as these.

(I immediately wondered whether I might not regret my offer. I couldn't help seeing that, in making it, I had put myself in Lazare's hands. Lazare had forgotten her disagreements with Michel. She wouldn't share his contempt for such a useful convenience. And nothing filled me with terror more than Lazare.)

I left Michel in a state of exasperation. I could not evade my inner feeling of guilt toward the workers. It was insignificant and indefensible, but it depressed me all the more because my guilt toward Lazare was of a similar kind. At such a time, I realized, my life had no justification. I was ashamed of this. I decided to spend the rest of the day and the following night at Calella. My urge to go slumming that evening abandoned me; on the other hand, I felt incapable of staying in my hotel room.

About twenty kilometers or so on the way to Calella (about half the distance), I changed my mind. There might be a cabled reply from Xenie at the hotel.

I went back to Barcelona. I had an unpleasant feeling. If the disturbances began, Xenie could no longer join me. So far, no answer had arrived. In a second telegram, I asked Xenie to do her utmost to leave that very evening. I no longer had any doubt that if Michel made use of my car, there was every chance that I would have to confront Lazare. I loathed the curiosity that was involving me, at a considerable remove, in the civil war. There was, unquestionably, no justification for me as a human being. Worst of all, my frenzy was useless. It was just after five o'clock, and the sun was scorching. Walking through the streets, I longed to talk to people. I was lost in the midst of an unseeing crowd. I felt no less stupid or helpless than a babe in arms. I went back to my hotel. There was still no reply to my telegrams. I felt an overpowering urge to mingle with the passersby and talk to them, but on the eve of the uprising this was impossible. I would have liked to know if there were any signs of unrest in the working-class neighborhoods. The city had an unusual air about it, but I was incapable of taking things seriously. I didn't know what to do, and I changed my mind two or three times. I decided at last to return to my hotel and lie down on the bed. There was something overly tense, excited, and at the same time dispirited about the entire city. I drove by way of Plaza de Catalunya. I was going too fast; a man who was probably drunk suddenly stepped in front of my car. I braked violently and managed to avoid him, but my nerves were shaken. I was sweating profusely. A little farther on, I thought I recognized Lazare in the company of Monsieur Melou, in gray jacket and straw hat. I was sick with dread. (Later, I learned that Monsieur

Melou had most definitely not come to Barcelona.)

At the hotel I declined to take the elevator and climbed the stairs. I threw myself onto one of the beds. I heard the sound of my heart inside my bones. I felt my veins beating, laboriously, in both temples. For a long time I lay sunk in spasms of expectancy. I splashed water onto my face. I was very thirsty. I then asked to be put through to Paris. There was no one in Xenie's apartment. I consulted a timetable and deduced that she might already be at the station. I tried my apartment, where, for the time being, during my wife's absence, my mother-in-law was still living. I thought that my wife might have returned. My mother-in-law answered. Edith had stayed in England with the two children. She asked me whether I had received the express letter — several days earlier, she had enclosed it in an envelope and forwarded it to me airmail. I remembered leaving a letter from her stuffed into one of my pockets: recognizing the handwriting, I hadn't opened it. I told her yes and hung up, irritated by the sound of an unfriendly voice.

The envelope, crumpled up in my pocket, was several days old. When I opened it, I recognized Dirty's handwriting on the express letter. Still uncertain, I feverishly began tearing open the flap. It was atrociously hot in the room. It was as though I would never finish tearing it open; I felt sweat trickling down my cheek. I glimpsed a sentence that horrified me, "I grovel at your feet." This, strangely enough, was how the letter began. What she wanted me to forgive her for was for not having had the courage to kill herself. She had come to Paris to see me. She was waiting for me to call her at her hotel.

I felt thoroughly wretched. For a moment I wondered — I had once again unhooked the receiver — if I would even know what to say. I managed to ask for the hotel in Paris. The waiting finished me off. I looked at the express letter: it was dated September 30. Today was October 4. In despair I started to sob. After a quarter of an hour, the hotel answered that Miss Dorothea S--- had gone out. (Dirty was merely an abbreviation — a provocative abbreviation — of Dorothea.) I left the necessary instructions. She could call me as soon as she returned. I hung up. It was more than my head could stand.

I was obsessed by emptiness. It was nine o'clock. In theory, Xenie was on the train to Barcelona, drawing rapidly nearer to me. I imagined the speed of the train, its lights vivid in the night as with a terrific din it drew nearer. I thought I saw a mouse, perhaps a cockroach — something black — cross the floorboards of the room between my legs. No doubt this was an illusion brought on by fatigue. I had a kind of dizzy spell. I was paralyzed, confined to the hotel, waiting for a phone call. There was no way of avoiding anything; the least initiative had been taken away from me. I went down to have dinner in the hotel dining room. I got up each time I heard the phone ring, afraid that the operator would

call my room by mistake. I asked for a timetable and
sent out for the newspapers. I wanted to know when
trains left Barcelona for Paris. I wanted to read the
Barcelona papers. I read, but without understanding
what I was reading. It occurred to me that, if necessary,
I could take the car as far as the border.

I was notified of a call while I was finishing dinner.
I was calm; but I suppose that, if someone had fired a
pistol next to me, I would barely have heard it. It was
Michel. He asked me to meet him. I told him that for
the time being that was impossible because of the phone
call I was expecting, but that if he was unable to stop by
the hotel, I would join him later that night. Michel gave
me the address where he could be found. He was determined to see me. He spoke like someone who has been
instructed to transmit orders and who is terrified of forgetting something. He hung up. I tipped the switch-
board operator, went back to my room, and lay down.
The heat in that room was excruciating. I drank a glass
of water from the tap: the water was lukewarm. I took
off my jacket and shirt. In the mirror I beheld myself
stripped to the waist. Once again I stretched out on the
bed. A knock on the door announced a telegram from
Xenie; as I had imagined, she would arrive next day on
the noon express. I brushed my teeth. I did not dare go
to the toilet for fear of not hearing the phone ring. I
tried to beguile the period of waiting by counting to five
hundred; I stopped halfway through. I thought: nothing
is worth getting into such a state of anxiety. Wasn't it a

blatant absurdity? Since the long wait in Vienna, I had not known anything so ruthless. At ten-thirty the phone rang; I found myself connected with the hotel where Dirty was staying. I asked to speak to her personally. I could not understand why she was having someone else speak to me. The connection was poor, but I managed to stay calm and speak clearly. As if, in this nightmare, I were the one calm presence. She had been unable to phone herself because the moment she came in, she had immediately decided to leave. She had barely had time to catch the last train to Marseilles. She would go by plane from Marseilles to Barcelona and arrive there at two in the afternoon. She had not had the time . . . it had been physically impossible for her to tell me herself.

It had never occurred to me for one second that I might be seeing Dirty the next day — that she might take the plane from Marseilles. As I sat there on the bed, I did not feel happy but almost dazed. I tried to remember Dirty's face — the beclouded expression of her face. My memory eluded me. I thought, she looks like Lotte Lenya; but the memory of Lotte Lenya in turn eluded me. I only remembered Lotte Lenya in *Mahagonny*: she wore a black, masculine suit with a very short skirt, a broadbrimmed straw hat, and stockings rolled down above the knees. She was tall and slender. I also remember her being red-haired. In any event, she was captivating. But the facial expression eluded me. I sat on the bed, in white trousers, bare foot and bare chested. I tried to remember the brothel song from the *Three Penny Opera*. I could not recall the German words, only those of the translation. I had the recollection — a mistaken one — of Lotte Lenya singing it. This vague recollection devastated me. I stood up on my bare feet and sang, in very low but devastated tones:

> And the ship with eight sails and
> Its fifty guns loaded
> WILL LAY SIEGE to the town....

I thought, tomorrow the revolution starts in Barcelona.... It was no good my being too hot: I was chilled to the bone.

I walked over to the open window. The streets were full of people. You could sense that the day had been one of broiling sun. There was more coolness outside than in my room. I had to go out. I slipped on a shirt and jacket, laced up my shoes as fast as I could, and took to the streets.

I went into a brightly lighted bar where I gulped down a cup of coffee. It was too hot, I burned my mouth. Drinking coffee, obviously, was a mistake. I went and took my car to go where Michel had asked me to meet him. I blew my horn; Michel would come down and open the front door of the building.

Michel kept me waiting. He kept me waiting for ages. I finally began hoping he wouldn't appear. No sooner had my car stopped in front of the designated building than I felt certain of having to confront Lazare.

I thought: Michel may loathe me, but he knows I'll do as he does — I'll forget the feelings Lazare arouses in me the moment circumstances demand it. He had every reason to believe this since I was, fundamentally, obsessed with Lazare: in my stupidity, I wanted to see her again. At that point I felt an overwhelming need to embrace my entire life in a single moment: the whole absurdity of my life.

But the situation looked bad. I would be reduced to sitting in a corner and not saying a word, no doubt in a room full of people, like an accused person summoned to appear and then mercifully forgotten. There would certainly be no opportunity for me to express my feelings to Lazare; she would only imagine that I felt sorry and ascribe my insults to illness. I suddenly had another thought: Lazare might find the world more bearable if disaster befell me. She must sense a crime in me that demands atonement. . . . She will be inclined to involve me in some nasty business: even if she is aware of the fact, she can decide that it's better risking a life as disillusioning as mine than that of a worker. I imagined myself being killed, and Dirty learning of my death at the hotel. I was at the wheel of the car. I put my foot on the ignition; but I didn't dare press down on it. On the contrary, I blew the horn several times and comforted myself with the hope that Michel would not appear. I had reached the point where I felt obliged to carry through whatever it was that fate offered me. In spite of myself, I envisioned Lazare's serenity and her undeniable daring with a kind of admiration. I could no longer take the business seriously. To my mind, it made no sense. Lazare surrounded herself with people like Michel who didn't know how to aim a gun and who shot the way they scratched. Nevertheless, she had the ability to make decisions, as well as the virile resoluteness of an organizer. I laughed as I thought how, on the other hand, the only talent I had was for losing my head. I thought back to what I had read about the terrorists. For the past few weeks, my life had estranged me from any concerns resembling those of the terrorists. The worst thing, obviously, would be to come through at a time when I would be acting not according to my own passions but Lazare's. In the car, as I waited for Michel, I gripped the steering wheel. I was like a trapped animal. I was dumbfounded by the idea that I *belonged* to Lazare, that I was in her possession.... I remembered that, as a child, I was as dirty as Lazare. The memory was painful. I recalled one depressing moment in particular. I was a boarder at a *lycee*. I used to while away my study hours, just sitting there, scarcely moving, often with my mouth hanging open. One evening, under the gaslight, I raised my desk top in front of me. No one could see me. I had grasped my pen and, holding it in my clenched right hand like a knife, I repeatedly buried the steel nib in the back of my left hand and forearm. Just to see — just to see, and also: *I wanted to inure myself to pain.* I inflicted a number of dirty cuts, more blackish than red because of the ink. The small cuts were crescent-shaped, like the nib seen in cross section.

I got out of the car and thus beheld the starry sky
overhead. Twenty years later, the boy who used to stick
himself with pens was standing under the sky in a for-
eign street where he had never been, waiting for some
unknown, impossible event. There were stars: an infin-
ity of stars. It was absurd — absurd enough to make
you scream; but it was a hostile absurdity. I was eager
for daybreak and sunrise. I reckoned that when the stars
disappeared I would surely be out in the streets. In
general I was less afraid of the starry sky than of the
dawn. I would have to wait, wait for two hours.... I remembered: it was about two in the afternoon, beneath a
brilliant Paris sun, and I was standing on the Pont du
Carrousel, when I saw a butcher's van drive past. The
headless necks of flayed lambs protruded from canvas
coverings; the butchers' blue-and-white striped smocks
were spotlessly clean; the van was slowly moving forward in open sunlight. When I was a boy, I loved the
sun; I used to shut my eyes and let it shine redly through
my lids. The sun was fantastic — it evoked dreams of
explosion. Was there anything more sunlike than red
blood running over cobblestones, as though light could
shatter and kill? Now, in this thick darkness, I'd made
myself drunk with light; and so, once again, Lazare in
my eyes was merely a bird of ill omen; a dirty, trivial
bird. My eyes were no longer lost among the stars that
were shining above me actually, but in the blue of the
noon sky. I shut them so as to lose myself in that bright
blueness. From it, fat black insects spouted forth in
buzzing swarms: just as, next day, there would emerge

at the blazing high point of the day, at first as an imperceptible speck, the plane that was bringing Dorothea.... I opened my eyes. The stars were still covering my head, but I was maddened with sunlight. I felt like laughing: next day, that plane, too small and distant to attenuate the sky's blaze even minimally, would appear to me in the likeness of a noisy bug; it would be harboring Dirty's preposterous fantasies inside its glassed-in cage; and as I stood there on the ground, it would, to my tiny human mind — at a moment when pain would be rending deeper than habit within her — assume the aspect of an impossible, adorable "outhouse fly." — So I had laughed, and it was no longer merely the gloomy boy with his cruel pen who was walking through the night hugging the walls: I had laughed the same laugh as a child, convinced that one day, since such a lucky insolence was sustaining me, it was I who was bound to turn the world upside down — turn the world, quite ineluctably, upside down.

3

I no longer understood how I could have been afraid of Lazare. If, after a few minutes' wait, Michel did not appear, I would leave. I was convinced he wouldn't come; it was an excess of conscientiousness that kept me waiting. I had almost decided to go when the front door of the building opened. Michel came over to me. He looked, to tell the truth, like a man from the other world; like someone who has shouted himself silly. I told him I was about to leave. He said in reply that the discussion "up there" was so chaotic and noisy that no one could make himself heard.

I asked him, "Lazare's there?"

"Naturally. She's the cause of it all.... There's no point in your going up. I've had it. I'll come and have a drink with you."

"Should we talk about something else?"

"No. I don't think I could. I'm going to tell you —"

"Right. Say what's on your mind."

I had only a vague desire to know. Michel seemed ludicrous to me at this point, and what was happening "up there" even more so.

"They're planning a surprise attack, with about fifty men — real gunslingers, you know the type. It's no joke. Lazare wants to raid the prison."

"When? If it's not tomorrow, count me in. I'll bring weapons. I can take four men in my car."

Michel shouted, "It's ridiculous!"

"Oh?" I burst out laughing.

"We shouldn't attack the prison. It's absurd!"

Michel had been speaking at the top of his lungs. We had come to a crowded street. I couldn't help saying to him, "Don't shout so loud."

He was taken aback. He stopped and gazed about him. A look of anxiety passed over his face. Michel was nothing but a child and a scatterbrain.

I laughed and said to him, "It doesn't matter. You were speaking French."

Reassured as quickly as he had been frightened, he in turn started laughing. But he did no more shouting after that. He even dropped the contemptuous tone in which he spoke to me. We were at a sidewalk cafe, where we picked a table off to one side.

He told me how he felt: "Let me explain why we shouldn't attack the prison. There's no point to it. If Lazare wants to take the prison by surprise, it's not because it's useful but because it suits her ideas. Lazare is revolted by anything resembling warfare, but since she's crazy, she favors direct action all the same. So she wants to mount a surprise attack. I suggested raiding an arms depot. She didn't want to hear about it, because the way she sees it, that means succumbing to the old confusion between revolution and war. You don't know what people are like here. People here are great, but they're nuts — they listen to her!"

"You haven't told me why you shouldn't assault the prison."

Basically, I was fascinated by the notion of assaulting a prison, and I liked the fact that the workers were listening to Lazare. The horror that Lazare inspired in me had abruptly vanished. I thought, she's gruesome, but she's the only one who understands. The Spanish workers understand the revolution, too.

Speaking for his own benefit, Michel had gone on with his explanation: "It's obvious. The prison is no use to anyone. What we need primarily is weapons. The workers must be armed. If the separatist movement doesn't put weapons into the hands of the workers, what's the sense to it? The proof is that the Catalanist leaders are probably going to lose out because they tremble at the thought of putting weapons into the hands of the workers. It's perfectly obvious: we should first raid an arms depot."

Another idea occurred to me: that they were all raving lunatics.

I began thinking of Dirty again. I myself was dead from exhaustion, full of anxiety once again.

Distractedly I asked Michel, "Which arms depot?"

He appeared not to have heard.

I insisted. It was a question he knew nothing about, although it was a basic, an embarassingly basic one; but he didn't know Barcelona.

"Has Lazare gotten any further?"

"Yes. She has plans of the prison."

"Would you rather we talked about something else?"

He kept quiet for a moment, not saying a word. He then went on: "I think it will turn out badly. The general strike has been called for tomorrow morning, but everyone will go his own way, and they'll all get wiped out by the civil guards. I'll end up believing that it's Lazare who's right."

"What do you mean?"

"That's it. The workers will never join forces, and they'll get beaten."

"Is taking the prison by surprise impossible?"

"How should I know? I'm no soldier...."

I was exasperated. It was two o'clock in the morning. I suggested meeting at a bar on the Ramblas. He would come when things were more definite. He said he would be there around five o'clock. I almost told him how wrong he was to oppose the prison venture, but I'd had enough. I walked Michel back to the door where I had waited for him and where I had parked the car. I was glad at least not to have met Lazare.

4

I went at once to the Ramblas. Leaving the car behind, I entered the *barrio chino*. I wasn't after women, but at night the *barrio chino* was the only way of killing time for three hours. At that hour I could listen to the men from Andalusia, the singers of *cante jondo*. I was beside myself from aggravation, and the aggravations of *cante jondo* were the one thing that might suit my feverishness. I went into a squalid tavern. As I entered, a woman on the verge of deformity — a blond woman with a face like a bulldog's — was performing on a small stage. She was practically nude; the colored handkerchief around her loins failed to conceal the deep black of her pubis. She was performing a belly dance and singing. I had barely sat down when another woman, no less hideous, came to my table. I was obliged to have a drink with her. The place was very full. It was pretty much the same crowd as at La Criolla, but shabbier. I pretended to speak no Spanish. Only one of the women was pretty and young. She looked at me. Her curiosity had the appearance of sudden ardor. She was surrounded by freaks whose charwomen's heads and bosoms were wrapped in filthy shawls. A young boy, hardly more than a child, dressed in a striped sailor's shirt, with curly hair and rouged cheeks, approached the girl who was gazing at me. He was wild-looking. He made an obscene gesture, burst out laughing, then went and sat down elsewhere. A very old, stooped woman with a peasant handkerchief over her head came in with a basket. A singer appeared and sat down on the stage with a guitar player. After a few measures from the guitar, he started to sing, in the most toneless manner possible. At that point, I might well have dreaded his singing the way the others do and devastating me with his cries. The room was large. At one end, a certain number of women were sitting in a row, waiting for customers to dance with. They would dance with the customers as soon as the singers finished their numbers. These girls were fairly young, but ugly and shabbily dressed. They were thin and undernourished. Some were dozing; others were grinning stupidly; others abruptly struck the stage with rapid little taps of their heels, while simultaneously uttering solitary *oles!* One of them, in a half-faded, pale-blue cotton dress, had a thin, blanched face beneath stringy hair: she would plainly be dead in a few months. I needed to stop thinking about myself, at least for the time being. I needed to think about other people and reassure myself that inside his own skull each was alive. I stayed there without speaking for nearly an hour, watching my fellow humans in that room. Afterward I went to another nightclub, which was, in contrast, very lively. An extremely young worker in overalls was spinning round and round with a woman in an evening gown. The evening gown revealed the dirty straps of her slip, but the woman was desirable. There were other spinning couples....I quickly decided to leave. I couldn't have stood any further excitement whatsoever.

I went back to the Ramblas and bought cigarettes and several magazines. It was barely four o'clock. Seated at a sidewalk cafe, I leafed through the magazines without seeing them. I tried to think of nothing; I couldn't manage to. Meaningless dust was billowing inside me. I would have liked to remember Dirty as she really was. What my memory vaguely recollected was something within me, something impossible, appalling, and above all alien. The next moment I would childishly imagine going and eating with her in one of the restaurants on the harbor. We would eat all sorts of spicy things I liked, then we would go to the hotel. She would sleep; I would stay near the bed. I was so tired that at the same time I thought of sleeping alongside her, in an armchair, even stretched out on the bed. Once she had arrived, we would both of us fall sound asleep; obviously, we would sleep badly. Then there was the general strike: a big bedroom, a candle, and nothing to do; empty streets; street fighting. Michel would be showing up at any moment. I must waste no time getting rid of him.

I would have liked to hear no more talk about anything. I felt like sleeping. The most urgent business people might tell me would go out the other ear. I had to go to sleep — fully dressed, anyplace. I must have fallen asleep several times in my chair. What to do when Xenie arrived. A little after six, Michel arrived and told me that Lazare was waiting for him on the Ramblas. He couldn't sit down. Their plans had fallen through. He seemed as distracted as I was. He felt no more like talking than I did; he was disheartened and half-asleep.

I immediately said to him, "I'm coming with you."

Day was breaking. The sky was pale, and there were no more stars. People were coming and going, but the Ramblas seemed somehow unreal: from one end to the other, that stretch of plane trees was one deafening birdsong — I had never listened to anything so unexpected. I caught sight of Lazare walking under the trees. Her back was toward me.

Michel asked me, "You don't want to say hello to her?"

At that moment, she turned around and started walking back in our direction, dressed in her everlasting black. For a moment I wondered if she weren't the most humane being I had ever seen. What was approaching me was also a monstrous rat. Not running away was what was necessary, and easy. I was, in fact, far away; I was very far away. I simply said to Michel, "You can leave, both of you."

Michel apparently did not understand. I shook hands with him and added (I knew where they both were

staying), "Take the third street on your right. Call me
tomorrow night, if you can" — as if Lazare and Michel
had together lost the merest shadow of existence. There
was no more authentic reality in me.
     Lazare looked at me. She could not have been more
natural. I looked at her and waved to Michel.
     They left.

     I went my own way toward my hotel. It was about
six-thirty. I did not draw the shutters. I soon fell asleep,
but it was a fitful sleep. I had the feeling it was daytime.
I dreamed I was in Russia; I was visiting one of the two
capitals as a tourist, most likely Leningrad. I was walking inside a huge iron-and-glass edifice that looked like
the old *Galerie des Machines*. Day had just broken, and
a dirty light was filtering through the dusty panes. Above
the dirt floor the empty space was more vast and more
solemn than a cathedral. I was depressed and utterly
alone. Through a side aisle I reached a series of little
rooms where mementos of the revolution were kept.
The rooms did not constitute an actual museum, but in
them the decisive episodes of the revolution had taken
place. They had originally been created for the life —
noble and fraught with solemnity — of the court of the
Czar. During the war, several members of the imperial
family had entrusted a French painter with the task of
depicting on the walls a "biography" of France. In the
austere, rhetorical style of Lebrun, he had narrated historical scenes from the life of Louis XIV. At the apex of
one wall, France was rising into the air with a ponderous

floorlamp in one hand. She seemed to be emerging from a cloud or a pile of wreckage, but she had, already, almost disappeared: the artist's work, casually sketched in places, had been interrupted by the uprising. The walls thus recalled a mummified Pompeian who, fully alive when the rain of ashes struck him, was *deadest* among the dead. Only the shouts and stamping of the insurgents still hung in the room, where breathing was difficult and came, so vivid was the terrifying abruptness of the revolution, in spasms or hiccups.

The adjoining room was the most oppresive. Its walls bore no trace of the old regime. The flooring was dirty and the plaster bare, but the advent of the revolution was recorded in numerous charcoal inscriptions. These had been drawn by the sailors or workers who, during the time they ate and lived in the room, had felt obliged to set down in crude language and cruder images the event that had overturned the universal scheme of things, and that their exhausted eyes had witnessed. I had never seen anything more irritating, or anything more human. I stood there, gazing at that crude, clumsy writing, and the tears came to my eyes. Revolutionary fervor slowly filled my head, sometimes expressed in the word "lightning-bolt," sometimes in the word "terror." Lenin's name frequently recurred in these inscriptions which, although traced in black, were more like traces of blood. The name was curiously altered; it had a feminine form — *Lenova!*

I left the little room. I entered a great, glassed-in
nave, aware that at any moment it would explode; the
Soviet authorities had decided to raze it. I couldn't find
the door, and I feared for my life. I was alone. After an
anxious moment, I saw an opening I could reach, a kind
of window set into the glasswork. I pulled myself up and
only with great difficulty managed to worm my way
outside.

I was in a desolate landscape of factories, railroad
bridges, and empty lots. I was waiting for the explosion
that would, with a single blast, upheave from end to end
the dilapidated building out of which I had emerged. I
had got clear of it. I went toward a bridge. It was then
that a cop started chasing me, together with a gang of
ragged children. The cop was evidently responsible for
clearing people from the area of the explosion. As I ran,
I shouted to the children which way to run. We reached
the bridge together. I then said to the children, in Rus-
sian, "*Zhdyes, mozhno*...We can stop here." The children did not answer. They were excited. We looked at
the building — it was visibly exploding (but we heard no
sound: the explosion released dark smoke, which did
not expand in swirls but rose straight toward the clouds
like crewcut hair, without the slightest shimmer; everything was irremediably dark and dusty....) There was a
stifling chaos, neither glorious nor grand, which dissi-
pated aimlessly as the winter night came on. It was a
night without even frost or snow.

I woke up.

I lay stretched out, in a stupor, as though the dream
had emptied me. I stared absentmindedly at the ceiling
and through the window at a section of bright sky. I had
a sense of escape, as if I had spent the night on a train in
a packed compartment.

Little by little, I began remembering what was happening to me. I leaped out of bed. I dressed without
washing and went out into the street. It was eight o'clock.

The day was beginning magically. I was aware, as I
stood in the sun, of the coolness of the morning. But my
mouth tasted foul; it was more than I could stand. Although in no way concerned with the answer, I asked
myself why this flood of sunlight, air, and life had
brought me onto the Ramblas. Everything was alien to
me; I had shriveled up, once and for all. I thought of the
bubbles of blood that form over the hole a butcher
opens in a pig's throat. I had one immediate concern: to
gulp down whatever might end my bodily nausea; then
shave, wash, and brush my hair; and, finally, go out
into the streets, drink chilled wine, and walk in the sunlight. I gulped down a cup of *cafe au lait*. I didn't have
the heart to go back to my room. I had a barber shave
me. Once again I pretended not to know any Spanish; I
expressed myself through signs. As I emerged from the
barber's hands, my zest for existence returned. I went
back and brushed my teeth as fast as possible. I wanted
to go swimming at Badalona. I took the car. I reached
Badalona around nine. The beach was deserted. I undressed in the car and, without lying down on the beach,
went into the water at a run. I stopped swimming and

looked up at the blue sky, toward the northeast — where
Dorothea's plane would soon appear. When I stood up,
the water came to my stomach. I saw my legs, yellowish
in the water, my two feet in the sand, and, out of water,
my torso, arms, and head. I felt an ironic curiosity in
seeing myself — in seeing what this thing was on the sur-
face of the earth or sea, this nearly naked character who
was waiting for a plane to emerge several hours later
from the depths of the sky. I started swimming again.
The sky was vast and pure; and, there in the water, I
would have liked to laugh.

5

As I lay face down in the middle of the beach, I
started thinking seriously about what to do with Xenie,
who would be first to arrive. I told myself that I should
waste no time getting dressed and dash off to the station
to wait for her. Since the night before, I hadn't forgotten the insoluble problem created by Xenie's arrival; but
each time I thought of it, I postponed its solution. Perhaps I wouldn't be able to make up my mind until I was
with her. I didn't want to be brutal with her any more —
at times I had behaved like a brute with her. I felt no
remorse, but I couldn't stand the thought of keeping it
up. The worst had ended for me a month earlier. Since
the night before, it seemed almost as though the nightmare were starting again — but I felt that it hadn't, this
was something else, I might even be coming to life. I

smiled now whenever I thought of the corpses, or of Lazare — all the things that had been hounding me. I went back into the sea, and on my back I had to shut my eyes: for an instant I felt as though Dirty's body had merged with the light and, especially, the heat — I became stiff as a stick. I felt like singing. But nothing seemed solid to me. I felt weak as an infant's cry, as if my life, now that it was no longer unhappy, were in its swaddling clothes — a puny thing.

The only thing to be done with Xenie was to meet her at the station and take her to the hotel. But I wasn't capable of having lunch with her. I couldn't think of an explanation to give her. I thought of calling Michel and asking him to have lunch with her. I recalled that in Paris they had occasionally seen one another. Crazy as that might be, it was the only possible solution. I got dressed. I phoned from Badalona. I had little confidence in Michel's accepting. Then he was on the other end of the wire; he accepted. He started talking to me. He was thoroughly discouraged. He spoke with the voice of someone in a slump. I asked if he resented my blunt treatment of him. He felt no resentment. At the time I had left him he had been too tired to think about anything. Lazare hadn't discussed anything with him. She had even asked him about me. I found Michel's attitude inconsistent: how could a serious activist, today of all days, be having lunch with a rich woman at a fashionable hotel! I tried to reconstruct logically what had happened late that night. I imagined that Lazare, together with Michel, had been eliminated by their own friends, partly because in Catalonia they were alien French, partly because among the workers they were alien intellectuals. I later found out that their affection and respect for Lazare had led them to agree with one of the Catalans, who proposed excluding her on the grounds that, being a foreigner, she knew nothing about the conditions of the working-class struggle in Barcelona. They were obliged to exclude Michel along with her. In the end, the Catalan anarchists with whom Lazare was associated kept to themselves but accomplished nothing: they relinquished all collective undertakings and confined themselves on the following day to sniping individually from the rooftops. As far as I was concerned, I wanted just one thing: for Michel to have lunch with Xenie. In addition, I hoped they would get along well enough to spend the night together; but it was enough, initially, for Michel to be in the hotel lobby before one o'clock, as had been agreed on the phone.

I belatedly recalled how Xenie used to proclaim her Communist views whenever she had the chance. I would tell her that I'd had her come down to be in Barcelona during the disturbances. She would be thrilled by the idea that I had judged her fit to take part in them. She would talk to Michel. However unconvincing this solution may have been, it satisfied me; I gave it no further thought.

Time passed very quickly. I went back to Barcelona. The city already had an abnormal air about it; cafes had taken away their sidewalk tables, stores had half-lowered their iron shutters. I heard a shot: a striker had fired through a streetcar window. There was a strange excitement, at times fugitive, at times oppressive. There was almost no car traffic. There were armed forces nearly everywhere. I realized that the car was a target for stones and shots. It was irritating not being out with the strikers, but I scarcely thought about it. The look of this city that was suddenly in need of an insurrection was agonizing.

I gave up the idea of returning to my hotel. I went straight to the station. No change had as yet been announced in the train schedules. I caught sight of the half-open door of a garage; I left the car there. It was only eleven-thirty. I had half an hour to kill before the train arrived. I found a cafe that was open. I asked for a carafe of white wine, but drinking gave me no pleasure. I thought back to the dream I had had that night about the revolution: I was more intelligent — or more humane — when I was asleep. I picked up a Catalan newspaper; but Catalan was a language I barely understood. The atmosphere in the cafe was pleasant and disappointing. Among the rare customers, two or three were also reading newspapers. In spite of everything, I had been struck by the ugly look of the streets downtown at the moment I'd heard a shot. I realized that in Barcelona I was on the fringe of things, while in Paris I was at their center. In Paris, during riot, I used to talk to anyone close at hand.

The train was late. There was nothing for me to do but walk up and down the station. The station looked like the *"Galerie des Machines"* through which I had wandered in my dream. Xenie's arrival annoyed me only slightly; but if the train was very late, Michel might start getting impatient at the hotel. It would be Dirty's turn to arrive in two hours; I would speak to her, she would speak to me, I would throw my arms around her. These possibilities, however, were beyond understanding. The Port Bou train pulled into the station. A few moments later I stood looking at Xenie. She had not yet caught sight of me. I watched her. She was busy with her luggage. She seemed quite short. She had thrown a coat over her shoulders, and when she tried to pick up her purse and a little suitcase, the coat fell to the ground. Stooping to retrieve her coat, she caught sight of me. I was on the platform; I was laughing at her. Seeing me laugh, she turned red; she burst out laughing herself. I took the little suitcase and the coat, which she handed to me through the train window. She could laugh all she liked — in my eyes she was an intruder, an alien. I wondered — dreading the idea — whether the same thing wouldn't happen with Dirty. Dirty herself would seem beyond my reach; Dirty, to me, was actually unfathomable. Xenie was smiling anxiously — she was feeling uneasy, and her uneasiness increased as she drew near and fell into my arms. I kissed her hair and forehead. It occurred to me that if I hadn't been waiting for Dirty, I would have been happy at that moment.

I was determined not to tell her that things between

us were going to be different from what she thought.
She saw how preoccupied I was. She was touching; she
said nothing, she simply looked at me — she had the eyes
of one completely in the dark and devoured by curiosity. I asked her if she had heard about recent events in
Barcelona. She had read something about them in the
French papers, but she had only a vague idea.

I said to her gently, "A general strike began today.
Something will probably start happening tomorrow.
You're just in time for the street fighting."

"You're not angry?"

I think I gave her an absentminded look. She was
twittering like a bird. She kept asking me, "Is there
going to be a Communist revolution?"

"We're having lunch with Michel T—. You can
talk to him about Communism, if you like."

"I hope there's a real revolution.... We've having
lunch with Michel T—? I'm exhausted, you know."

"We should have lunch first. Afterward you can
sleep. Stay right here for now. The taxis are on strike.
I'll be back with a car."

I left her standing there.

It was a complicated business — an absurd business. I found the role I was compelled to play with her
distasteful. Once again I was forced to treat her as I had
in my sickroom. I realized that I had attempted to escape my life by going to Spain, but that the attempt had
been pointless. What I had escaped had pursued and
caught up with me and was once again demanding that I

behave like a lunatic. I wanted at all costs to stop behaving that way, but in spite of this, Dirty's arrival would make everything turn out for the worst. I walked rather quickly through the sunshine toward the garage. It was hot. I mopped my face. I was jealous of people with a God to hang onto, whereas I...soon all I'd have left would be "eyes to cry with." Someone was staring at me. My eyes had been lowered; I looked up: it was a beggar, in his thirties, who wore on his head a bandana tied under his chin and broad yellow goggles across his face. He stared at me out of his big eyes for a long time. In the sunshine, there was an insolent look about him — a sunlike look. I thought, "Perhaps it's Michel in disguise!" That was childish nonsense. This strange beggar had never before laid eyes on me.

After I had walked past him, I abruptly turned round; he was staring at me harder than ever. I tried imagining what his life was like. There was something irrefutable about that life. I myself might turn into a beggar. In any case, *he* was one; he was one for *life*, and nothing else: this was the fate he had latched on to. I'd latched on to something a little gayer. I came back from the garage the same way. He was still there. Once again he stared at me. I drove by slowly. It was hard for me to let go of him. I would have liked to have that dreadful look, that sunlike look of his, instead of acting like a little boy who never knows what he wants. It then occurred to me that I might have been happy living with Xenie.

She was standing at the station entrance, her suitcases at her feet. She didn't see my car coming. The sky was bright blue, but everything was happening as though a thunderstorm were about to break. Surrounded with suitcases, her disheveled head lowered, Xenie looked as though the ground were collapsing beneath her. I thought: later today, it will be my turn, eventually the ground will collapse beneath me as it has beneath her. Drawing level with her, I gazed at her unsmilingly, with a look of despair. She was startled seeing me; at that moment her face revealed her anguish. She recovered as she approached the car. I went to get her suitcases. There was also a batch of periodicals — picture magazines and *L'Humanite.* (Xenie had come to Barcelona by sleeper, but she was reading *L'Humanite!)*

Everything happened quickly. We barely spoke before reaching the hotel. Xenie gazed out at the city streets, which she was seeing for the first time. She said that at first glance Barcelona struck her as a lovely city. I showed her the strikers and riot troops massed in front of one building.

She immediately said to me, "Why, that's dreadful!"

Michel was in the hotel lobby. He came rushing up with his usual awkwardness. Xenie obviously interested him; he had come to life on seeing her. Scarcely hearing what he was saying, she went up to the room I had arranged for her.

I explained to Michel, "I have to go now. Can you tell Xenie that I'm leaving Barcelona by car until tonight, but without specifying what time?"

Michel told me I wasn't looking well. He seemed troubled himself. I left a note for Xenie: I said that I was frantic because of what was happening to me. I had been completely in the wrong where she was concerned, I had wanted to behave differently now — since last night, that was impossible. How could I have foreseen what would happen to me?

As I spoke to Michel, I repeated that I had no personal reason for worrying about Xenie, but she was very unhappy; the thought of leaving her alone made me feel like a criminal.

I dashed out, sick at the thought that someone might have wrecked the car. No one had touched it. Fifteen minutes later I reached the airfield. I was an hour early.

6

I was like a dog straining at the leash. I saw nothing. Confined by time, by the moment, by the throbbing of my blood, I felt the pain of a man who has been tied up to be killed and is trying to burst his bonds. I expected no further happiness. What I might expect, I could know nothing about — Dorothea's life was too wild. A few moments before the plane's arrival, with every hope ruled out, I grew calm. I was waiting for Dirty, I was waiting for Dorothea the way a man waits for death. The dying man suddenly realizes that it's all over: what will shortly happen, however, is the one thing in the world that ever mattered. I had grown calm, but the arrival of the low-flying plane was abrupt. I ran toward it. I didn't see Dorothea at first, she was behind a tall old man. At first I wasn't sure that it was her. I drew nearer. She had the thin face of an invalid. She had no strength left and had to be helped down. She saw me, did not look at me — she let herself be carried, unmoving, with lowered head.

She spoke to me, "Just a moment —"
I said to her, "I'll carry you in my arms."
She did not answer, she submitted, and I lifted her up. She was skeletally thin. She was clearly in pain. She was limp in my arms, no less indifferent than if a hired man were carrying her. I settled her in the car. Seated in the car, she looked at me. She smiled an ironic, acid smile — an unfriendly smile. What did she have in common with the woman whom, three months before, I had watched drinking with an apparently unquenchable thirst? Her clothes were yellow — sulfur-colored, the same color as her hair. I had long been haunted by the idea of a sunlike skeleton, of sulfur-colored bones. Dorothea was now a wreck. Life seemed to be forsaking her.

She said to me softly, "Let's hurry. I have to be in bed as soon as I can."
She was done in.
I asked her why she hadn't waited for me in Paris.
She seemed not to have heard but finally answered, "I'd done enough waiting." She was staring sightlessly in front of her. At the hotel, I helped her out of the car.

She wanted to walk as far as the elevator. I took her arm, and we made our way forward. In the bedroom I helped her undress. She told me in a low voice what had to be done. I must avoid hurting her; I gave her whatever linen she wanted. As I undressed her and her nakedness appeared (her shrunken body was less *pure*), I couldn't help suppressing a grim smile; it was better having her sick.

She said, with a kind of relief, "The pain's gone. But I have no strength left at all."

I had not touched her with my lips, she had scarecely looked at me, but what was happening in the bedroom was bringing us closer.

Once she had stretched out on the bed, with her head centered on the pillow, her features relaxed. She soon looked as beautiful as before. For a moment she gazed at me, then looked away.

The shutters in the bedroom were drawn, but rays of sunlight were drifting through them. It was hot. A maid came in with a bucket of ice. Dorothea suggested I put ice in a rubber bag and lay the bag on her belly.

She told me, "That's where it hurts. I lie flat on my back with some ice."

She spoke to me again, "I was out yesterday when you called. I'm not as sick as I seem."

She smiled; but her smile was unsettling.

"I had to travel third class as far as Marseilles. Otherwise I would have left tonight at the earliest."

"Why? Didn't you have enough money?"

"I had to keep some for the plane."

"Was it the train ride that made you sick?"

"No. I've been sick for a month, the jolts only hurt. I was in pain, in great pain, all through the night. But —"

She took my head in both hands and looked away as she told me, "The pain made me happy."

No sooner had she spoken than the hands that had reached out for me pushed me to one side.

But never since our first meeting had she spoken to me in this way.

I got up. I went into the bathroom and cried.

I came back immediately. I assumed an aloofness to match hers. Her features had hardened — as if she felt obliged to avenge herself for her avowal.

A surge of passionate, inaccessible hatred gripped her. "If I weren't sick, I wouldn't have come. Now I'm sick and we're going to be happy. I'm sick at last."

A grin disfigured her in her repressed fury.

She became hideous. I realized that I loved this violent impulse in her. What I loved in her was her hatred: I loved the sudden ugliness, the dreadful ugliness that hate stamped on her features.

7

The doctor I had sent for was announced. We were asleep. The unfamiliar, half-darkened room in which I woke up seemed empty. At the same moment Dorothea also woke up. She started when she saw me. I was sitting up in the armchair — I was trying to think where I was. I was unsure about everything. Was it nighttime? It was daytime, obviously. I unhooked the ringing phone. I asked the front desk to send the doctor up.

I waited for him to finish examining her. I felt utterly dejected, scarcely awake.

Dorothea had some woman's trouble. In spite of the seriousness of her condition, she might recover fairly rapidly. The trip had made things worse; she shouldn't have traveled. The doctor would be back. I took him to the elevator. As he was leaving, I asked him how things were going in Barcelona. He said that as of two hours ago the general strike had been total — everything had come to a stop. But the city was calm.

He was an insignificant man. I don't know why I said to him, smiling stupidly, "The calm before the storm..."

He shook hands with me and went off without replying, as though I had no manners.

Dorothea was relaxed. She combed her hair and put on lipstick.

She said, "I'm better. What was it you asked the doctor about?"

"There's been a general strike. There may be a civil war."

"Why a civil war?"

"Between the Catalans and the Spaniards."

"A civil war?"

The idea of a civil war bewildered her. I told her once again, "You must do what the doctor said —"

I was wrong to mention it so soon. It was as though a shadow had passed; Dorothea's face became inaccessible.

"Why should I get well?" she said.

Chapter 5 • *The Feast of the Dead*

D¹orothea had arrived on the 5th. On October 6, at ten in the evening, I was sitting next to her while she told me what she had done in Vienna after leaving me.

She had gone into a church.

There had been no one inside. At first she had knelt on the flagstones, then lain face down, stretching her arms crosswise. It meant absolutely nothing to her. She didn't understand why she had done it, but after a while a series of thunderclaps had jolted her. She had gotten up and, leaving the church, set out at a run beneath the downpour.

She had taken shelter in an archway. She was hatless and wet. There was a young boy wearing a cap in the archway, a very young boy. He wanted to joke with her. In her despair, she was incapable of laughing. She had drawn close and kissed him. She had felt him; he

had responded by feeling her. She had lost all control —
she had terrified him.

She was relaxed as she spoke to me. She said, "It
was like a younger brother — he smelled wet, and so did
I, but I was in such a state that when he came he was
quivering with fright."

At that point, as I listened to Dorothea, I had forgotten about Barcelona.

We heard a bugle sound quite nearby. Dorothea
stopped short. She listened, surprised. She began speaking again, then fell wholly silent: there had been a volley
of shots. There was a moment's respite before the shooting started up again. It came suddenly pouring forth,
not far away. Dorothea had sat upright. She wasn't
afraid, but there was a tragic abruptness about it. I went
to the window. I saw people armed with rifles shouting
and running under the trees on the Ramblas, which that
night were dimly lighted. The firing was coming not
from the Ramblas but from adjacent streets. Snapped
off by a bullet, a branch fell.

I told Dorothea, "This time it's serious."

"What's happening?"

"I don't know. It must be the regular army attack-
ing the others." (The others were the Catalans and the
Generalitat of Barcelona.) They were shooting on Calle
Fernando: that was right next to us.

A wild salvo shook the air.

Dorothea went over to one of the windows. I turned

round. Shouting, I said to her, "You're crazy. Go right back to bed."

She was in man's pajamas. She was barefoot and unkempt. Her face looked cruel.

Pushing me aside, she looked out the window. I showed her the broken branch on the ground.

She turned back towards the bed and took off her pajama top. Naked to the waist, she began looking around her. She seemed insane.

I asked her, "What are you looking for? You've absolutely got to go back to bed."

"I want to get dressed. I want to go out with you and see."

She seemed out of control. She was wild and inaccessible, she spoke unanswerably, cresting on some kind of fury.

At that moment someone started beating on the door with his fists. Dorothea threw down the pajama top she had removed.

It was Xenie. I had told her everything the day before, when I left her with Michel. Xenie was trembling. I looked at Dorothea; I found her provocative. She was standing there, bare breasted, silent, and mean.

I told Xenie curtly, "You have to go back to your room. There's nothing else to do."

Without looking at her, Dorothea interrupted me, "No — you can stay, if you like. Stay with us."

Xenie, in the doorway, did not move. The firing went on. Dorothea tugged me by the sleeve. She led me to the far end of the room and spoke into my ear.

"I just had a horrible idea — understand?"

"What idea? I don't understand anything. Why invite the girl to stay?"

Dorothea stepped away from me. There was a sly look about her, and at the same time, she was obviously at the end of her tether. The noise of rifle-fire was mindshattering. Her eyes lowered, her voice aggresive, she spoke to me again, "You know I'm an animal!"

The other could hear her.

I rushed over to Xenie and beseeched her, "Get out, right now."

Xenie herself was beseeching me. I retorted, "Do you understand what will happen if you stay?"

Staring at her, Dorothea laughed cynically. I pushed Xenie toward the corridor; as she struggled, Xenie kept sullenly insulting me. She had been frantic from the start and, I was sure, sexually beside herself. I kept shoving, but she went on struggling. She started yelling like a demon. There was such violence in the air — I pushed her with all my might. Xenie went crashing down, straddling the corridor. I bolted the door. I had lost my self-control. I too was an animal, but I had also been trembling — I had imagined how Dorothea might have taken advantage of my preoccupation with Xenie to jump out the window and kill herself.

2

Dorothea was exhausted; she let me lift her up

without a word. I put her to bed. She was submissive, limp in my arms, her breasts bare. I went back to the window. I drew the shutters. I was alarmed by the sight of Xenie outside the hotel. She was crossing the Ramblas at a run. There was nothing I could do. I couldn't leave Dorothea alone for one second. I saw Xenie head not toward the firing but toward the street where Michel was staying. She disappeared.

Disturbances continued through the night. Sleep was impossible. Little by little the intensity of the firing increased. Machine guns and later cannons began sounding. In the room where Dorothea and I were closeted, there might have been something grand in hearing this, but it was, above all, indecipherable. I spent part of the time walking up and down the room.

In the middle of the night, during a lull, I was sitting on the edge of the bed. I spoke to Dorothea.

"I don't understand your going into a church."

We hadn't spoken in a long time. She started, but she did not reply.

I asked her why she wasn't saying anything.

She answered that she had been dreaming.

"But what do you dream about?"

"I don't know."

A little later she said, "I can grovel at His feet if I believe He doesn't exist."

"Why did you go into the church?"

She rolled over and turned her back to me.

She then said, "You ought to go away. It would be better now if I stayed by myself."

"If you'd like it better, I can go out."

"You want to get yourself killed."

"Why? Rifles don't kill much of anyone. Listen — they never stop firing. That proves fairly conclusively that even the shells leave a large number of survivors."

She was following her own train of thought.

"It would be less dishonest."

At that point she turned toward me. She gave me an ironic look.

"If only you could let yourself go!"

I didn't blink.

3

During the following afternoon the street fighting, whose intensity had diminished, resumed sharply from time to time. During one lull, Xenie rang from the front desk. She was shouting into the phone. Dorothea was asleep at the time. I went down to the lobby. Lazare was there, trying to restrain Xenie. Xenie was disheveled and dirty. She looked like a madwoman. Lazare was as resolute and funereal as ever.

Escaping from Lazare, Xenie dashed at me as though she wanted to strangle me.

She kept screaming, "What have you done?"

On her forehead, bleeding from beneath a torn scab, was a large sore.

I took her by the wrists, twisting them to make her shut up. She was feverish; she was trembling.

Without letting go of Xenie's wrists, I asked Lazare what was happening. She said to me, "Michel just got himself killed. Xenie's convinced it's her fault."

I had to strain to hold on to Xenie; at the sound of Lazare's voice she had started struggling. She was making a fierce effort to bite my hands.

Lazare helped me hold on to her; she held her head. I was trembling myself.

After a while Xenie kept still.

She was standing in front of us panic-stricken. She said in a hoarse voice, "Why did you treat me like that? You threw mé down — like some kind of animal —"

I was holding her hand, and I squeezed it very hard.

Lazare went off to ask for a wet towel.

Xenie went on, "— with Michel, I was horrible. The way you were with me — it's your fault. *He* loved me. He was the only one in the world who loved me. I treated him ... the way you treated me. He lost his head. He went off and got killed.... Now, Michel's dead. It's horrible."

Lazare put the towel on her forehead.

We each held her by one arm and led her back to her room. She let herself be dragged along. I was crying. I saw that Lazare was starting to cry too. Tears were streaming down her cheeks. She was as self-possessed and funereal as ever, and it was abominable seeing her tears flow. We settled Xenie in her room, on her bed.

I said to Lazare, "Dirty's here. I can't leave her alone."

Lazare looked at me, and in that moment I saw

that she no longer had the heart to despise me. She simply said, "I'll stay with Xenie." I shook hands with Lazare. I even held her hand a moment in mine, but I was already thinking that it was Michel who was dead, not I, I then embraced Xenie: I would have liked to give her a real kiss, but I felt myself verging on insincerity. I left immediately. When she saw me going away, she began crying, but didn't make a move. I went out into the corridor. I was crying, too, by contamination.

4

I stayed in Spain with Dorothea until the end of October. Xenie went back to France with Lazare. Dorothea was getting better from day to day. I used to take her out in the sunshine during the afternoon (we had gone to live in a fishing village.)

At the end of October we had no money left. Neither one of us. Dorothea had to return to Germany. I was to take her as far as Frankfurt.

We reached Trier on a Sunday morning, the first of November. We had to wait for the banks to open next day. It was an afternoon of ,rainy weather, but we couldn't stay cooped up in our hotel. We walked through the countryside up to a height that overhung the Moselle valley. It was cold; rain was starting to fall. Dorothea was wearing a gray cloth traveling coat. The wind had rumpled her hair; she was damp with rain. At the edge of town we asked directions from a respectable little man with a big mustache and a derby hat. With disconcerting kindness, he took Dorothea by the hand and led us to the crossroads where we could get our bearings. He went away and then turned back and smiled at us. Dorothea herself gazed after him with a disillusioned smile. Since we hadn't listened to what the little man had said, a little farther on we made a mistake. We were obliged to walk for a long time, far from the Moselle, in neighboring valleys. The earth, the stones of the sunken path, and the bare rocks were bright red; there were frequent woods, plowed lands, and meadows. We crossed a yellowing wood. Snow began falling. We met a group of Hitler Youth, children ten to fifteen years old wearing shorts and black velvet boleros. They walked fast, paid no attention to anyone, and spoke in abrupt voices. There was nothing that wasn't dismal — terribly so: a vast gray sky slowly turning into falling snow. We started moving fast. We had to cross a plateau of plowed earth. Freshly worked furrows proliferated; and above us the snow, endlessly borne by the wind. Immensity surrounded us. Hurrying down a back road, our faces lashed by the wind, Dorothea and I felt we no longer existed.

We came to a restaurant with a tower on it. It was warm inside, but there was a squalid November light in the place, as well as numerous well-to-do families seated at the tables. Her lips pale, her face red from the cold, Dorothea said nothing. She ate a kind of cake she was fond of. She was still beautiful; nevertheless her face kept dissolving in that light, dissolving in the gray of the sky. On our way down we easily found the right path, which was very direct, laid out in switchbacks through the woods. It had stopped snowing, or almost had; the snow had left no trace. We walked quickly, slipping or stumbling from time to time. Night was falling. Farther down, in the half darkness, the city of Trier appeared. It stretched along the far bank of the Moselle, with high square towers rising above it. We little by little lost sight of these towers in the night. As we went across one clearing we saw a house, low but vast, surrounded by arbored gardens. Dorothea spoke of buying the house and living there with me. There was nothing left between us except disillusioned hostility. We could sense it: we mattered little to one another, not, at least, after anxiety abandoned us. We were hurrying toward a hotel room, in a city that we had never seen until the day before. In the darkness we sometimes reached out toward one another. We would look into one another's eyes, not without dread; we were bound together, but we no longer felt the slightest hope. At one turning in the path, an empty space opened beneath us. Curiously, this empty space, at our feet, was no less infinite than a starry sky over our heads. Flickering in the wind, a multitude of little lights was filling the night with silent, indecipherable celebration. Those stars — those candles — were flaming by the hundred on the ground: ground where ranks of lighted graves were massed. We were fascinated by this chasm of funereal stars. Dorothea drew closer to me. She kissed me at length on the mouth. She embraced me, holding me violently tight; it was the first time in a long while that she had let herself go. Leaving the path across plowed earth, we took the lover's dozen steps. We still had the graves below us. Dorothea opened wide, and I bared her to the loins. She in turn bared me. We fell onto the shifting ground, and I sank into her moist body the way a well-guided plow sinks into earth. The earth beneath that body lay open like a grave; her naked cleft lay open to me like a freshly dug grave. We were stunned making love over a starry graveyard. Each of the lights proclaimed a skeleton in its grave, and they thus formed a wavering sky, as unsteady as the motions of our mingled bodies. It was cold. My hands sank into the earth. I unbuttoned Dorothea, smirching her underclothes and breast, with the cold earth that stuck to my fingers. Emerging from her clothes, her breasts were of a lunar whiteness. We let go of one another from time to time, simply letting ourselves quiver with cold: our bodies were quivering like two rows of teeth chattering together.

The wind made a wild sound in the trees. I said to Dorothea in a stammer (I was stammering and talking wildly), "...My skeleton...You're shivering. Your teeth are chattering...."

I stopped and lay on top of her, heavy and still, panting like a dog. Abruptly I clasped her naked buttocks. I fell on her with my full weight. She uttered a terrific scream. I clenched my teeth as hard as I could. At that moment we began sliding down the sloping ground.

Farther down, the rock formed an overhang. If I hadn't stopped our slide with my foot, we would have fallen into the night, and I might have wondered with amazement if we weren't falling into the void of the sky.

I had to pull my pants up as best I could. I was standing up. Dirty was still on the ground, on her naked backside. She got up with difficulty, grasping one of my hands. She kissed my nakedness. Earth had stuck to the fur of my legs; she started scratching it off. She clung to me. She made teasing, sly gestures of extravagant indecency. At first she made me fall down. I had a hard time getting back up. I helped her to her feet. I helped her put her clothes back on, but it was difficult, with our bodies and clothes so earthy. We were as excited by earth as by naked flesh; no sooner was Dorothea's cleft out of sight under her clothes than I hurriedly bared it again.

On our way back, with the graveyard behind us, the streets of the town were empty. We passed through a neighborhood consisting of low dwellings — old houses separated by gardens. A little boy went by. He stared at Dirty in astonishment. She reminded me of the soldiers who fought the war in muddy trenches; but I was impatient to be with her in a heated room and take her dress off in the light. The little boy stopped for a better look at us. From her great height Dirty leaned down and made a horrible face at him. The ugly, well-to-do little boy disappeared at a run.

I thought of little Karl Marx and of the beard he had, later, when he grew up. He was underground now, near London — Marx must also have run through the streets of Trier as a little boy.

5

We had to go to Coblenz the next day. From Coblenz we took a train to Frankfurt, where I was to leave Dorothea. As we went up the Rhine valley, a fine rain was falling. The banks of the Rhine were gray, but stark and wild. From time to time the train skirted graveyards whose graves had disappeared under masses of white flowers. As night came on, we saw lighted candles on the graveyard crosses. We were to separate several hours later. Dorothea had an eight o'clock train heading south; a few minutes later, I would catch the train to Paris. Night fell after Bingerbruck.

We had a compartment to ourselves. Dorothea drew closer in order to talk to me. Her voice was almost childlike. She squeezed one of my arms very hard. She said, "There'll be a war soon, won't there?"

I answered softly, "I have no idea."

"I wish I knew. You know what I imagine sometimes: I imagine the war having started. And then I have to tell a certain man that war has broken out. I pay him a visit. Evidently he isn't expecting it; he turns pale."

"And?"

"That's all."

I asked her, "What made you think about the war?"

"I don't know. Will *you* be frightened if there's a war?"

"No."

She drew nearer to me, resting her burning forehead against my neck.

"Henri, listen — I know I'm a freak, but I sometimes wish there would be a war...."

"Why not?"

"You'd like it, too? You'd be killed, wouldn't you?"

"What made you think about the war? Was it because of yesterday?"

"Yes. Because of the graves."

For a long time Dorothea sat huddled against me. The previous night had exhausted me. I started falling asleep.

As I fell asleep, Dorothea — to keep me awake — began caressing me, slyly, almost without moving. She went on speaking softly, "You know, the man I tell about there being a war —"

"Yes."

"He looks a little like the man with the mustache — the one who took me by the hand in the rain. A really nice man, with lots of children."

"What about the children?"

"They all die."

"Killed?"

"Yes. And each time, I pay the little man a visit. It's ridiculous, isn't it?"

"You're the one who notifies him of the death of his children?"

"Yes. Each time he sees me he turns pale. I appear dressed in black, and you know, when I leave —"

"Yes?"

"There's a puddle of blood where I've been standing."

"What about you?"

Her breath issued from her like a moan, as if she were suddenly beseeching:

"I love you."

She pressed her cool mouth against mine. I was in a state of intolerable joy. When her tongue licked mine, it was so wonderful I might have wished my life over.

In my arms (she had taken off her coat), Dirty was in a bright red silk dress — the red of swastikaed flags. Her body was naked under the dress. She smelled of wet earth. I left her, partly out of excitement (I wanted to move around), partly to reach the end of the car. In the corridor I twice inconvenienced a very tall, very handsome SA officer. He had porcelain-blue eyes that even in a lighted railway car were lost in the clouds, as if he had personally heard the Valkyries' summons; but no doubt his ear was more attuned to the trumpet-call of the barracks. I stopped on the threshold of the compartment. Dirty switched on the night light. She was standing motionless, in a dim glow. She frightened me. Beyond her, in spite of the darkness, I saw a vast plain. Dirty was looking at me, but she herself was elsewhere,

lost in some horrible dream. I approached her; I saw
that she was crying. I clasped her in my arms. She refused to give me her lips. I asked her why she was crying.

I thought, no one can know her any less than I do.
She answered, "No reason."
She burst out sobbing.
As I embraced her, I felt her. I wished I were sobbing myself. I would have liked to know why she was
crying, but she had stopped speaking. I kept seeing her
the way she was when I came back to the compartment:
as she stood in front of me, she had the beauty of a
ghost. Once again I felt frightened of her. Smitten with
anxiety by the prospect of her leaving me in a few hours,
I suddenly thought: she's too voracious to go on living.
She won't live. From beneath my feet came the noise of
wheel on rail, of wheels that crush, in crushed, bursting
flesh.

The final hours passed quickly. In Frankfurt I
wanted to find a room. She refused. We had dinner together: the only way to endure was to have something to
do. The final minutes, on the platform, were unbearable. I didn't have the courage to go away. I was to see
her several days later, but I was possessed. I kept thinking that before then she would die. She disappeared with
the train.

I was alone on the platform. Outside, it was pouring. As I went off, I was crying. I had difficulty walk-

ing. In my mouth I still had the taste of Dirty's lips —
an inexplicable something. I began staring at one of the
railroad men. He went by; I felt sick looking at him.
Why was it he had nothing in common with a woman I
could kiss? He had eyes, a mouth, and a backside of his
own. That mouth made me want to retch. I would have
enjoyed hitting it; he looked like an obese, well-to-do
citizen. I asked him the way to the toilet (where I should
have been hurrying as fast as I could.) I hadn't even
wiped away my tears. He gave me directions in German,
it was hard understanding. I reached the far end of the
hall. I heard a sound of fierce music, a sound of unbearable bitterness. I was still crying. From the station entrance I saw in the distance, at the far end of a vast
square, a well-lighted stage and, on the tiers of the stage,
a cortege of uniformed musicians. The sound was magnificent, ear-rending in its exultation. I was so surprised
I immediately stopped crying. I no longer felt like going
to the toilet. In the driving rain I crossed the square at a
run. I took shelter under the projecting roof of the stage.

I was standing in front of children who were lined
up on the tiers of the stage in military formation. They
were in short black velvet pants and short jackets
adorned with shoulder knots; they were bareheaded;
fifes to the right, side drums to the left.

They were playing with such ferocity, with so stri-
dent a beat, that I stood breathless in front of them.
Nothing could have been more abrupt than the beating
of the side drums, or more caustic than the fifes. As
they faced the vast, empty, rain-drenched square and

played for occasional passersby, all these Nazi boys (some of them were blonde, with doll-like faces) seemed, in their sticklike stiffness, to be possessed by some cataclysmic exultation. In front of them, their leader — a degenerately skinny kid with the sulky face of a fish — kept time with a long drum major's stick. He held this stick obscenely erect, with the knob at his crotch, it then looked like a monstrous monkey's penis that had been decorated with braids of colored cord. Like a dirty little brute, he would then jerk the stick level with his mouth; from crotch to mouth, from mouth to crotch, each rise and fall jerking to a grinding salvo from the drums. The sight was obscene. It was terrifying — if I hadn't been blessed with exceptional composure, how could I have stood and looked at these hateful automatons as calmly as if I were facing a stone wall? Each peal of music in the night was an incantatory summons to war and murder. The drum rolls were raised to their paroxysm in the expectation of an ultimate release in bloody salvos of artillery. I looked into the distance. . .a children's army in battle order. They were motionless, nonetheless, but in a trance. I saw them, so near me, entranced by a longing to meet their death, hallucinated by the endless fields where they would one day advance, laughing in the sunlight, leaving the dead and the dying behind them.

Against this rising tide of murder, far more incisive than life (because blood is more resplendent in death than in life), it will be impossible to set anything but trivialities — the comic entreaties of old ladies. All things were surely doomed to conflagration, a mingling of flame and thunder, as pale as burning sulfur when it chokes you. Inordinate laughter was making my head spin. As I found myself confronting this catastrophe, I was filled with the black irony that accompanies the moments of seizure when no one can help screaming. The music ended; the rain had stopped. I slowly returned to the station. The train was assembled. For a while I walked up and down the platform before entering a compartment. The train lost no time in departing.

May, 1935

Appendix: The Author's Foreword [1957]

To a greater or lesser extent, everyone depends on *stories*, on *novels*, to discover the manifold truth of life. Only such stories, read sometimes in a trance, have the power to confront a person with his fate. This is why we must keep passionately striving after what constitutes a *story*: how should we orient our efforts to renew or, rather, to perpetuate the *novel*?

Many minds are no doubt preoccupied with various techniques that will compensate for the surfeit of familiar forms. But what is the point in this — assuming that we wish to find out what a novel *might* be — unless first of all a ground is ascertained and clearly delineated? A story that reveals the possibilities of life is not necessarily an appeal; but it does appeal to a moment of fury without which its author would remain blind to these possibilities, which are those of *excess*. Of this I am sure: only an intolerable, impossible ordeal can give an author the means of achieving that wide-ranging vision that readers weary of the narrow limitations imposed by convention are waiting for.

How can we linger over books to which their authors have manifestly not been *driven*?

It has been my aim to set forth this principal. I decline to justify it.

I shall simply list some titles that corroborate what I assert (only a few: I could list others, but haphazardness best reflects my intention): *Wuthering Heights, The Trial, Remembrance of Things Past, The Red and the Black, Eugenie de Franval, The Death Sentence, Sarrazine, The Idiot....*[1]

It has been my aim to express myself clumsily.

I do not mean to imply, however, that one burst of fury, or the endurance of suffering, is in itself enough to confer on stories the power of revelation. I have mentioned these things in order to be able to say that the freakish anomalies of *The Blue of Noon* originated entirely in an anguish to which I was prey. These anomalies are the ground of *The Blue of Noon*; but I was so far from assuming that this ground was a guarantee of quality as to refuse to publish the book, which was written in 1935. Friends who were affected by a reading of the manuscript have now urged its publication, and I have decided to leave the matter up to them. I had, however, more or less forgotten its very existence.

No later than 1936, I had decided to think no more about it.

In the meantime, moreover, the Spanish Civil War and the World War had rendered insignificant the historical events connected with the plot of the novel. Con-

---

[1] *Eugenie de Franval*, by the Marquis de Sade (in *Les Crimes de l'Amour*); *The Death Sentence* (*L'Arret de Mort*), by Maurice Blanchot; *Sarrazine*, a novella by Balzac, comparatively little known but one of his outstanding works.

fronted with tragedy itself, why pay any attention to its portents?

This reasoning suited the dissatisfaction and uneasiness that the book itself inspires in me. But those circumstances have now become so remote that my story, written as it were in the blaze of events, has now fallen into the same category as others, those which their authors have by deliberate choice set in an insignificant period of the past. Today I am far removed from the state of mind out of which the book emerged; this concern, however, which was originally a predominant one, is no longer relevant; and I have thus deferred to the judgment of my friends.

OTHER BOOKS OF INTEREST PUBLISHED BY URIZEN

LITERATURE

Bataille, Georges
Story of the Eye,
120 p. / Cloth $5.95

Bresson, Robert
Notes on Cinematography,
132 p. / $6.95 / paper $3.50

Brodsky, Michael
Detour, novel,
350 p. / Cloth $8.95

Cohen, Marvin
The Inconvenience of Living, fiction,
200 p. / Cloth $8.95 / paper $4.95

Ehrenburg, Ilya
The Life of the Automobile, novel,
192 p. / Cloth $8.95 / paper $4.95

Enzensberger, Hans Magnus
Mausoleum, poetry,
132 p. / Cloth $10.00 / paper $4.95

Hamburger, Michael
German Poetry 1910-1975,
576 p. / Cloth $17.50 / paper $7.95

Handke, Peter
Nonsense & Happiness, poetry,
80 p. / Cloth $7.95 / paper $3.95

Innerhofer, Franz
Beautiful Days, novel,
228 p. / Cloth $8.95 / paper $4.95

Kroetz, Franz Xavier
Farmyard & Other Plays,
192 p. / Cloth $12.95 / paper $4.95

Shepard, Sam
*Angel City, Curse of the Starving
Class & Other Plays,*
300 p. / Cloth $15.00 / paper $4.95

MOLE EDITIONS

Clastres, Pierre
Society Against the State,
188 p. / Cloth $12.95

Elias, Norbert
The Civilizing Process, Vol. 1 & 2,
400 p. / Cloth $15.00 each Vol.

Gibson, Ian
The English Vice,
364 p. / Cloth $12.95

Schivelbusch, Wolfgang
The Railway Journey,
275 p. / photos / Cloth $15.00

Sternberger, Dolf
Preface by Erich Heller
Panorama of the 19th Century
212 p. / Cloth $15.00

ECONOMICS

DeBrunhoff, Suzanne
Marx on Money,
192 p. / Cloth $10.00 / paper $4.95

Howard, Dick
The Marxian Legacy,
340 p. / Cloth $15.00 / paper $5.95

Linder, Marc
Anti-Samuelson, Vol. I,
400 p. / Cloth $15.00 / paper $5.95
Anti-Samuelson, Vol. II,
440 p. / Cloth $15.00 / paper $5.95

CONTEMPORARY AFFAIRS

Andrew Arato / Eike Gebhardt (Eds.)
*The Essential Frankfurt School
    Reader,*
554 p. / Cloth $17.50 / paper $6.95

Augstein, Rudolf
Preface by Gore Vidal
Jesus, Son of Man,
420 p. / Cloth $12.95 / paper $4.95

Burchett, Wilfred
Southern Africa Stands Up,
Cloth 12.95 / paper $4.95

Kristeva, Julia
About Chinese Women,
250 p. / Cloth $8.95

Ledda, Galvino
Padre, Padrone,
Cloth $9.95

Sartre, Jean-Paul
Sartre by Himself,
136 p. / photos / Cloth $10.95 / paper $3.95

Steele, Jonathan
Inside East Germany,
300 p. / Cloth $12.95

Stern, August
The USSR vs. Dr. Mikhail Stern,
420 p. / Cloth $12.95

Write for a complete catalog and send orders to:
Urizen Books, Inc., 66 West Broadway, New York, N.Y. 10007
212 - 962-3413